A dirty bo

– Author Unknown

DOWN and DIRTY 2

40 Explicit Fantasies to Rock the Libido

edited by Alison Tyler

Published by Accent Press Ltd – 2008
ISBN 9781906125912

Printed and bound in the UK by
Creative Design and Print

Cover Design by
Red Dot Design

Twelve new titles for 2008

Bad Girl

Seriously Sexy One

Naughty Spanking One

Tease Me

Down and Dirty One

Seriously Sexy Two

Juicy Erotica

Satisfy Me

Naughty Spanking Two

Seriously Sexy Three

Down and Dirty Two

Seduce Me

For more information please visit
www.xcitebooks.com

Contents

Introduction

If there were an award for touching yourself, for making yourself come while all alone, I would win hands down. All right. Not exactly hands "down," but hands working, caressing, stroking, touching and playing … Hands knowing exactly what to do to take me to my outer limits of pleasure.

You see, I am an expert at "solo style."

Some people might think that masterful masturbation is all about technique. That anyone can come if touched just right. And they're correct, to a point. You have to know where your erogenous zones are, and how to manipulate them, in order to reach the elusive finish line. Lotions can help. As can sex toys or pictures in a magazine. But in my opinion, the most powerful muscle to exercise when in the quest for coming is your mind. And as a frequent solo-style performer, I have one hell of a fantasy-filled brain.

I like to think of my dirty thoughts as different books filling the "erotic library" in one large X-rated corner of my mind. When in search of a good time all by myself, I close my eyes and rifle through the shelves until I find precisely what I'm looking for, not unlike someone standing bent over in front of the fridge, rummaging for the perfect satisfying late-night snack. But instead of in some dimly lit kitchen, I'm in my head, my fingers trailing over the backs of the glossy-bound books, remembering each different fantasy by the titles on the spines:

• The X-School: Where naughty pupils are taught a lesson by one strict teacher. (Sometimes the teacher is male, sometimes female. Sometimes *I'm* the teacher.)

• The Petting Zoo: A public place to watch other people masturbate. I can play the voyeur, or the exhibitionist.

• An Erotic Examination: A visit in which a doctor teaches a patient precisely how to come by giving her a step-by-step instruction. I like to play both roles.

• The Club: At a private, underground club, it's clothing optional and sex mandatory!

My fantasies are not alphabetised, and they don't always remain exactly where I leave them on the shelves. Sometimes, I can't even find the precise one that I'm looking for. I'll remember a tidbit – was it about a movie star? Johnny Depp? Richard Gere? Or was it a scenario – somebody was getting a spanking, right? Or maybe being fucked in the shower? Given an examination? Sucking cock? But I won't be able to recreate the whole story from scratch. Maybe this is because my collection is incredibly vast. I am quite the erotic connoisseur.

So just how many fantasies line the walls of my dirty library?

I couldn't possibly tell you. They've been gathering up there for nearly twenty years now. Some are one-time reads that I probably won't venture back to again; others grow worn with use, frequent favourites that I return to again and again. You might think I wouldn't ever want to reuse one more than once, but that's just not true. My favourite fantasies are revisited repeatedly, bringing me promised pleasure every time.

Occasionally, fantasies have grown and changed as I've matured, myself. But some remain pristine, like Snow White in her glass box, never altered, never added to, because they work just fine. God, they work great. I have fantasies that push the limits, and some that are very tame. I own ones I'd never share with anyone, not even my partner of eight years, and some that my lover could recite for you in perfect detail. Every so often, my fantasies have been sparked from actual events – while some never happened, even remotely, and never will.

My favourites?

One stars a heavyset driver who delivered beauty products to the store where I worked way back when. (Think James Gandolfini if you want the body type.) He finds me playing with myself in the upstairs stockroom where I'm supposed to be organising lipsticks, and he administers a deliciously firm spanking before fucking me against the wall.

In another, I'm at a sleep-over party with several of my adult girlfriends. After the rest of the ladies fall asleep, I make my way into the master suite and make love to the hostess' husband while the other girls sleep peacefully in each other's arms.

You want more?

I'm in empty bar wearing only a shorty nightgown. I can see it perfectly: it's grey flannel and it barely reaches the tops of my thighs. A man I've never met before enters the building. He's wearing a white shirt, jeans with a belt. He's handsome in a severe way, with blue eyes and brown hair. He bends me over a tall barstool and whips me with the leather until I cry, and then he fucks me.

Not satisfied? That's OK. There's more. There's always, endlessly more …

I'm stopped at a traffic light and I look over to catch the gaze of a young guy in the truck next to my car. He follows me to a deserted alley, and we screw like animals in his truck bed, never exchanging names.

In another, I'm at a sex toy shop in New York city.

3

The fine dyke behind the counter explains the various uses for the different toys, after binding my wrists with a pair of $500 silver cuffs. (Did I say that she explains the uses while using me as a willing demonstrator?)

Still more? Well, I'm happy to oblige. You see, that was the reason I collected the fantastic stories for this book: to give readers a range, a library of sexual adventures to return to again and again.

As for me, I have to go …

You see, I'm entered in this contest, and I think I just might win for the solo-style event.

Your editor, as ever,

Alison Tyler

A Girl In Coveralls
by Thomas S. Roche

You're under the Chevy, dressed in blue short-sleeve coveralls, filthy with grease. I stand there in the doorway watching you, getting more and more turned on. There's something so hot about the way you work that lug wrench. Your hands tighten around the handle, gripping it, stroking it as you turn. You don't realise I'm watching; you just go about your business. When you climb out from under the car, you go around to the cabinet to get the jack. You fit the device under the fender and fondle the jack handle for a moment, making sure it's turned at the right angle to fit into the tiny slot.

You push the jack handle home and crank it once. I've come up behind you without being seen. My hand closes on yours, stopping you.

You gasp.

"Fuck, you scared me," you say, and I grasp the back of your coveralls, guiding you to your feet, facing away from me. I push you hard over the hood of the car, eliciting another gasp. I force you down so your breasts push hard against it, and draw my hand up the back of your shapely thigh. I stroke the curve of your hips through the well-washed, threadbare industrial fabric, and I realise you're not wearing anything underneath.

"There's something so hot about a girl in coveralls," I

tell you, and I force your legs apart just a little and press my hand between your legs. You moan, pushing your ass up into the air, clutching at the hood of the car but not finding purchase. I reach around you and grab the top of your coveralls. I pull so hard the snaps come undone and the zipper starts to tear. I grab the zipper and pull it down all the way to your crotch, exposing your tits. My hands mold to them, kneading and pinching.

"Fuck," you gasp as I squeeze your nipples. I move my hands back to the open front of your coveralls and pull down firmly. You obediently put your arms back and the coveralls come easily off your shoulders, exposing your upper body completely. I slide them over your hips and the worn blue fabric goes sinking down to your ankles, pooling around the work boots you're wearing. Your ass is bare underneath, your legs open just enough that your pussy is exposed. I reach between your legs and feel it as I press your naked upper body to the well-waxed hood of the vintage Chevy. You're incredibly wet already — whether from working on the muscle car or from my rough, insistent caresses, I'll never know. I drop down behind you, hand on the small of your back to keep you pressed forward. Your legs aren't spread wide enough for me to get my face between your thighs, so I slide two fingers into you and mold my mouth to the narrow cleft between your cheeks. You gasp as my tongue presses unexpectedly against your asshole. I work your clit with one hand while I fingerfuck you with the other and push my tongue more firmly against your back door. The vintage muscle car crackles as you thrash so hard on the hood that even the '70s-era Detroit steel distends under the pressure. I drive my tongue deeper into your ass and press more firmly against your clit. I hear you moaning, begging for more.

I ease my fingers out of your pussy, my tongue out of your ass. I slide up behind you and unfasten my jean shorts, pulling out my cock.

When the head of my cock nuzzles against your pussy, you lift your ass higher to give me better access. At this angle, with the coveralls keeping your legs from spreading fully, I know it will be a tight angle. When I slide into your cunt, you press your body back against mine and I feel the tightness of your entrance. You moan as I start to fuck you. Your arms are spread out above you on the hood of the muscle car, the butch mechanic suddenly helpless at the feel of a hard cock. I slide in deeper and reach under you to rub your clit.

"Oh God," you gasp. "Fuck …me …"

I pound you faster, feeling the harness of the car underneath us, knowing your thighs and my shins are going to be covered in bruises. But neither of us cares; you, in particularly, *clearly* don't care what kind of bruises you have. You lift your ass for me and push back onto my cock with each thrust. You beg me to fuck you harder, and I do.

When you come, I hear the thunder of your fists against the hood of the Chevy. You shudder all over and your pussy clenches around my thrusting cock. You're so tight at this angle that the spasms of your orgasming cunt push my cock out of you for a moment, and when I force it back in with great difficulty, it only makes you moan louder and come harder. I have to hold deep inside you, hands on your hips, positioning you just right, to keep fucking you through the violent spasms of your climax.

Then it grabs me unawares, my own orgasm, exploding through my balls and into my cock, pulsing through my whole body, my cock spurting deep inside you as I groan. When I slump, exhausted, on top of you, I hear the "chunk" of protest from the tortured Chevy hood.

"There's something so sexy about a girl with her hands on a muscle car," I whisper into your ear.

Your fingers absently stroke the smooth hood of the Chevy, caressing it lovingly.

Maybe You Should Spank Me
by Gwendolyn J. Mintz

Michael was home already. I could hear him in the kitchen, fiddling around between the refrigerator and stove. When I walked in, he glanced up.

"Hey Babe," I said, dropping my purse and files on the counter. I gave him a kiss on the cheek, but he didn't respond.

"Long day?" I asked.

He shrugged. "Just that big meeting. Needed to look professional …"

I stared at him blankly until I remembered. His lucky tie! I was supposed to have taken it to him during lunch.

"Oh, Michael, I'm sorry."

Michael shrugged and turned back to whatever it was he was preparing.

I watched in silence as he turned off the stove and spooned his food onto a plate. "Did you get the deal?"

"Yeah," he said, "but that's not the point.

I agreed. "I didn't mean to forget."

"OK," he murmured.

The look on his face broke my heart. I opened my mouth several times, but I didn't know what to say. I apologised again because I felt bad. Then with an unexpected brainwave, I teased, "Maybe you should me spank me."

Michael moved to the table and pulled out a chair. He glanced over at me.

"Got a lucky belt? Or maybe just your hand?" What the hell was I saying?

He set the plate down and considered me for awhile.

"Maybe I should," he said, taking my arm and pulling me toward him. He sat, laying me out across his lap.

"Hey, just kidding," I protested, trying to get up, though I was aware of a warmth building between my legs at the thought.

His hand pressed at the small of my back, pinning me firmly to his lap.

Then he roughly lifted the hem of my dress. Though I was stunned, I raised my hips to help him. When he slipped his hand into the back of my panties, his palm grazing my skin, I did what I could to kick them off.

"Oh, you want this – don't you?" Michael asked. I hardly recognised his voice.

Though his tone was accusatory, I realised, that yes, I did want it. I said nothing. Just waited, my ass quivering in anticipation.

Whack!

"Oh," I said, with an intake of breath. Then as the sensation spread, I uttered something closer to a moan.

His hand came down several times in quick succession.

A flaming sensation blazed across my cheeks, but it wasn't entirely one of pain. I squirmed against my husband, grinding myself into his lap, feeling him grow hard beneath me.

"Be still," Michael barked.

He ran his palm across and down my ass. I opened my legs.

"I didn't say you could do that," Michael hissed, his

hand smacking my ass again and again. "Gonna behave?" he asked.

My vision blurred. I clung to the legs of the chair. It wasn't so much fun anymore. I croaked out a "yes."

"Maybe I'm not done," he said, dipping his hand between my legs and slipping two of his fingers into me.

I suppressed the moan threatening to escape. I swear I heard slippery noises with his every stroke. When he withdrew his fingers, I let out a dark sigh of protest. I glanced up at him. He inched his fingers into his mouth, pulled them out, and pushed them in. Catching my eyes, he raised his brows and winked at me. "The taste of punishment."

I squirmed.

Michael's hand again. Whack!

"You want more?"

I whipped my head from side to side. "No more spanking," I whimpered.

"You want me to stop?"

My head bobbed up and down.

"But what if I don't think you've been punished enough?"

My brain reeled. "If you stop," I whispered, "I'll go down on you."

Everything in the kitchen except for the yellow-framed clock fell silent. Our breathing kept time with the tick, tick. I could hear the Murrays' dog barking in their backyard. Looking at the floor, I could see the shadow of Michael's arm, suspended in air.

"What … did … you say?" He wanted me to repeat the words. He wanted to relish each one. Like so many men, Michael craved oral sex more frequently than he ever got it. 24 hours a day wouldn't have been enough.

Now, I looked up over my shoulder and grinned at

11

him, chose my words carefully. "I will suck your cock," I offered.

Michael got a glassy-eyed, eager look. His mouth fell and I as well as he stood abruptly.

"Sorry," he mumbled, helping me to my feet. "For real?" he asked.

"Oh yes," I promised. Something had stirred inside me. I ran my tongue across my top lip. Then bit the lower.

Michael's face glowed.

"Beat you to the shower," I said.

It was only seconds before the two of use raced to the bathroom, discarding clothes on the way.

I was open for whatever else might happen. And who knew? Just maybe that "lucky tie" might get used today after all.

Passing Notes
by Lea Bricker

Construction noises sounded through the window as the professor started his meaningless droning on about dates and events two hundred years old. It was hot in the room – broken air conditioning – and Rachel wished she were able to remove a few more items of clothing. As it was, she was wearing very little, in cut off shorts and a tank top. Summer classes were certainly the worst, she concluded. Who could concentrate in this heat?

She was taking half-hearted notes, doodling in the margins of her notebook, when a piece of folded up paper was slipped under her arm. It had her name printed on it. Looking around, she saw no one paying attention to where the note had ended up. She shrugged and opened it.

I show up at your door with a single red rose in my hand. You answer in nothing but a black bra and thong set, with a garter belt and stockings. You smile and beckon to me to come inside.

Rachel looked up again, scanning the room wildly. Again, no one was paying any attention to her, nor did she recognise the writing. Who had given her this strange note? And why? Did she dare reply to it? Hell. She was bored, and why not. She picked up her pen and continued:

13

I take the rose and kiss you on the cheek, saying that I need to put it in water, which I do. You watch my nearly bare ass as I walk into the kitchen. When I return I see that you have sat down on the sofa and made yourself comfortable with the television. I take the remote from you and cast it aside before I straddle your hips.

She folded it up and passed it back the way it had come. Watching, it disappeared into the throng of students. The paper returned a few minutes later. *You grind your hips into mine and we start moving together. You lean down to kiss me — gently — but I attack your mouth and you melt into me. I am getting very excited by your presence.*

I can feel your arousal and toy with the zipper of your jeans, simply to frustrate you. You squirm under me, so I climb aside and sit next to you, driving you even more insane.

The paper came back to her. "You are truly evil. Sometimes naughty little girls need to be punished. Would you like to be punished?"

She almost laughed. Who was this person? She blended her reply back into the prose.

"Yes, I want to be punished," I whisper into your ear. My tongue darts out and licks your ear lobe.

Well then, I pull you onto my lap, facedown on the couch, your lovely little bottom up in the air. I trace the edges of your stockings with my fingertips, lightly running them up the garter straps and over your ass. I caress you softly.

One of Rachel's hands was resting on her lap, and she found her fingers attempting to rub herself through her cut-offs.

I sigh happily and grind my pussy into your lap.

You've got me so worked up with anticipation.

I have you fully enraptured when I bring down my palm, spanking you only hard enough for it to sting. I do this several times, then stoke your reddening skin. Slipping my hand down between your legs I feel that you've become very wet over a few spankings.

You keep your hand between my legs, pulling aside the tiny strip of fabric covering my pussy ...

God, she couldn't believe she was writing this out of boredom – and enjoying it way too much!

You slip a finger between my wet folds fingering my clit. I moan and push myself against you.

I smile and run the fingers of my free hand through your hair as I continue to fondle your clit. When I push a finger inside of you, you gasp in surprise. I work your clit as I finger you, moving in and out slowly as you rock your hips.

Despite my want, I sit up and start unbuttoning your shirt. You help me along, and you are soon down to just your underwear. My face is level with your waist.

I pull down my boxers – I always wear boxers – and my hard cock is finally free. You take it into your hand and pump it a few times. "Oh God," I mutter. You grin and then kiss the head of it gently. I beg for more.

I tell you to lie down on the couch. Leaning over you I slowly draw you into my mouth, swirling my tongue over the head, sucking gently. Your hips buck at the sensation, which I call as my cue to suck harder. After a moment or two I get on the couch as well, straddling you in the 69 position.

I lick the insides of your thighs, slowly working my way up to your central core. I have to concentrate very hard, because your mouth on my penis is driving me insane. The second the tip of my tongue touches your clit you grind down on me, fucking my face. I lick and suck eagerly, and you do the same.

You feel so good, I want to scream. Your tongue laps at my juices, and I am going insane. Your fingers find a way back into me and I push myself against you, wanting. I feel everything building up inside of me. I start to shake as I orgasm, grinding into your face even harder. When you pull away, you suggest we go upstairs to my bedroom. I agree breathlessly.

Rachel was very much in need, and wished class was over, desperate to find a bathroom and relieve herself. She had never once considered masturbating in a public place, but didn't care. She sent the paper back, now on its second page.

I grab at your ass as we go upstairs and you giggle. Once upstairs, I throw you on the bed. I slip your sopping wet underwear off, but leave the stockings and bra on. I like them. I move my hands over your breasts, then follow with kisses. My hands slip down over your stomach and part your legs, revealing your pretty pink nether lips.

I reach down and stroke your erection, making it so hard it's like brick. "I want you to fuck me," I say softly. "Please. Fuck me hard."

Rachel looked up as she passed it back and realised

16

that people were getting up to leave. Class was over, and she had no idea what the lecture had been about. The letter came back one more time as students started to file out the room.

I straddle your hips an place the head of my cock at your opening. I push in slowly ... TO BE CONTINUED.

Happy Birthday
by Simone Harlow

Maris Landry unlocked the front door of her house. She shoved her keys in her purse, kicked the door shut, then slammed her purse on the hall table, unholstered her service weapon and put it on the table. Her handcuffs came next, then her detective shield. After pulling the velcro tabs on her bullet-proof vest, she yanked it over her head, and dropped it on the floor.

Happy Fucking Birthday to me.

She started stripping in the hall, dropping clothes as she walked to her bedroom. She needed a shower, a Scotch, Cherry Garcia and bed. In that order.

After showering and single malt, she earned her menage a trois with the most dependable men in her life, Ben and his buddy Jerry. The whole pint, no spoonful and calling that dessert. Tonight she was licking the carton clean.

Shoving a spoonful in her mouth, she heard the doorbell ring. This had better not be her sister, Angela wanting to celebrate her birthday. Maris would shoot her. As she headed to the door, her phone rang. She grabbed the cordless. "I'll be right there," she yelled at the door.

"Hello?"

"Happy Birthday, baby sister. How's thirty-five?"

"It sucks." She adjusted her robe. "You at the door?"

"No, but your birthday present is."

Her sister was into the S&M scene. And she just swore Maris needed to join her. "What did you get me? Leather chaps? A giant dildo? I'm sending it back."

"What did you tell me you wanted this year?"

She thought for a minute. "A twenty-year-old named Nick." Maris peeked out of the window. From her angle she could see was a blond head. Oh shit. "You got me a guy?"

Angela laughed. "Not just any guy. I sent you Nick."

Maris opened the door. There in the door way stood a blond god. Naked. Except for the big red bow hiding his stuff. "Oh my God."

"Happy Birthday," Angela yelled.

Behind naked guy, Maris saw her neighbour's front door open. She grabbed Nick's arm and pulled him inside and slammed the door. As a cop, she dealt with a lot of freaky shit, but it never followed her home before. She was gonna cap Angela as soon as she got rid of naked Nick.

"Do you like him?"

What's not to like. A face like an angel, a bod built for sin. She liked him just fine. "I said young, dumb and hung. He ain't young." She lifted his right hand. "I see a West Point ring. Class of 94. The Point means he's not dumb."

"He's younger than you."

Maris lifted up the bow. His long thick cock stood at attention like a good soldier. Her warrior cometh. "Oh my."

"One out of three ain't bad." Angela cackled.

Soldier boy Nick grinned.

She dropped the bow. "Can't you at ease that thing."

Nick shrugged. "He likes you."

19

God help her she was turned on. "Your name really Nick?"

He held out his hand. "Nicolas Bennett."

Maris ignored his hand. "Are you one of her …" What was the word she called her dates?

"Her pet? No I'm not a pet."

Angela laughed. "He lost a bet and he's mine for a night. I thought you needed him more than I did."

Maris was not amused. "Thanks."

"Don't mention it, sis."

Maris gripped the phone tighter. Her sister had gone too far. "Call me next year and maybe I won't be mad at you."

"I'll see you at Mom's on Sunday. Enjoy your present."

Maris disconnected and put the phone in her robe pocket. She squared her shoulders. Her cop face on, she took a step closer to Nick. "My pint of Ben and Jerry's is getting lonely, get your naked behind out of my house."

He crossed his arms over his massive chest. "No."

"Don't bust a 'tude with me Big Dick Nick." Maris put her hands on her hips. "I'm LAPD, I'll kick your ass."

A blond eyebrow raised. "I'm ex Special Forces. So, no … you won't."

The fact that Nick's finely rippled body, was standing between her and her gun, put a new slant on the picture.

"You want me."

She did. He was walking fuck fantasy. "You showed up. Ha ha, big surprise. Now go." She tried to sound convincing.

"I always pay my debts."

Wonder what he bet on. "What did you bet on?"

He didn't answer, he ripped off the bow and stood before her glorious naked.

Maris turned her head, not wanting to stare at the package. Gawking was totally uncool. She needed to keep her pride. "Put that thing away."

He took a few steps and slung her over his shoulder. "Let's play." He started walking up the stairs.

"I'm not into this shit." Although this caveman routine was kinda sexy.

"We'll see."

Her stomach bounced on his shoulder all the way up the stairs. This was a chance for her to get a gander at his ass. It was high and firmly muscled. He had the Renoir's of butts. This beat the Glock 28, her dad bought her last year.

Happy Birthday to me.

Nick tossed her on the bed. For a second she just lay there. There was defiance in her brown eyes. He liked that. She wouldn't be easy to tame, but she would be fun. He leaned over and slid his hand between her legs until he felt her hot damp pussy. As his fingers sunk into her moist slit, she bit her full bottom lip. Her back arched and one on lush breasts slipped free of her red silk robe. Well rounded and full, he noticed she had nicely perky nipples. "Still wanna kick my ass, Detective?"

She shook her head.

He smiled pushing his finger inside her. Instantly he felt her muscles clinch around his finger. "I didn't think so." With his free hand, he untied the sash of her robe and pushed the material aside. Her high firm breasts would fit into the palms of his hands perfectly. She had a strong fit body she kept combat ready. She had fight in her. He liked that. Nick squeezed the two white globes and then bent to lick them.

Maris whimpered as her legs spread wider.

21

"Good girl." Nick went to his knees. He took his finger out of her pussy. He spread her legs wider and knelt down inside her legs. He had to taste her. Nick started tonguing her with broad flat strokes, licking her entire snatch. Her juices flowed. He grabbed her hips to stop her from wiggling as his tongue flicked over her hard clit. His cock grew harder as he pushed his tongue inside her as deep as it would go.

Nick couldn't stand not having his cock inside her. Lifting up her legs, he hooked them over his shoulders. Slowly he guided his cock into her exposed opening. His instinct was to conquer and subvert, but Maris needed a gentle hand. Anything but a straight fuck and he'd lose her.

She was so tight, he only managed to get the head of his cock into her damp pussy.

"Please."

"Easy, baby you're tight." He entered an inch at a time. The strain was destroying him, he clamoured for release. Sweat beaded on his body. Using his thumb, he pulled back on the hood of her clit and began to massage her hard nub.

She drove her hips up and forced his cock in deeper. She began to ripple in climax. Nick knew it was impossible for him to wait to come and he impaled his straining cock inside her to the hilt. He pumped inside her hard and fast. He felt her climax around him once more. Harder and harder he drove into her until he was ready to burst. Her tight pussy milked his cock as he exploded inside her. Nick dropped her legs and fell to his knees. His head land on her stomach. He inhaled, her skin smelled like jasmine and sex. "Happy Birthday, Maris."

Maris ran her hand through his damp hair. "You're a

keeper."

Nick laughed, and it was clear from his expression that he agreed.

Phone Sex
by Simon Keen

His phone buzzed. It was set to vibrate only but it did so loud enough to be heard by everyone in the meeting. He knew from the single buzz that it was a text message.

"Sorry," he said, feigning embarrassment, as he took his phone from his pocket and read the message.

I am sitting on the sofa naked. I want you to fuck me.

His face did not show any emotion as he read the message from his wife. He looked back up at the others to assure them they had his full attention, which they didn't. As he did so he switched his phone to silent, he was expecting more text messages to appear.

There were three other men and one woman in the room. They were all in their early 40s, about five years younger than him. All busy discussing an upcoming exhibition at the NEC and what the company would show on its stand. The woman looked across at him showing obvious signs of interest as to what it was that had deflected his attention.

He lowered his phone into his lap, keeping it in one hand. He was adept at using the keys to send text messages even when not looking, proving that this was not merely the territory of teenagers. While he looked across the table he typed out his reply, glancing down a couple of times to make sure he had not mis-keyed.

I am in a meeting and it would be more fun if you were here then I could fuck you on the board room table in front everyone.

Her phone buzzed as his reply came in. She did not need her phone on vibration only but she had it tucked up against her naked pussy and enjoyed the sensation. She lifted the phone and opened her legs as she read his reply.

Her eyes shut and she conjured up a picture in her mind of walking into his meeting naked and laying herself out on the table. They didn't make love in public and neither wanted to but it was different in a fantasy. In a fantasy you are allowed to do anything and it is always good.

As she lay back on the sofa with her fantasy growing she let her hand stray down to her pussy which was already becoming hot and moist. Another message came in and added to her dream.

I would invite everyone to look at your lovely pussy and to taste it.

She could see everyone looking at her checking her out; each one bending down to run their tongue the full length of her pussy. All were men but the last one to touch her was a woman. As the woman stood over her she felt herself flush, half with embarrassment and half with anticipation. In real life she had never slept with a woman but this was not real life. The woman crouched down to the edge of the table and just touched the tip of her tongue against her erect clitoris. As she did this the woman slipped her finger between buttocks moist with juice. The woman slid her finger into a firm but well lubricated arse. In her mind she felt the woman's well manicured nail, it was sharp but in a fantasy things don't hurt. As the mental image of the woman's tongue flicked across her clit so did her finger in the real world.

25

I wouldn't let them have too much though. *While you were being licked I would get my secretary to stroke and suck my cock to make it very hard for you.*

She saw him standing beside the table with a young woman sucking his cock. She wanted his cock hard and ready to fuck her. The sight of her husband's cock being sucked turned her on immensely and she rubbed her clit harder and faster.

Then I would fuck you whilst everyone watched. I might let them wank and come all over you.

She opened her eyes long enough to read the last message and then disappeared back into her dream. He was fucking her on the table. She was surrounded by men wanking furiously over her. She looked sideways and saw the one woman being riding one of the men. At this she came but still kept rubbing wanting to come again, imagining her husband still fucking her. As he came so did she.

She lay there on the sofa her eyes shut, the edge of the cushion wet with her juice. Eventually she stirred, opening her eyes and trying to move. She wanted him beside her, holding her. She wanted to feel his cock and smell his cum.

Don't be late tonight I want you inside me.

When he received the reply he knew she had come. That she had rubbed her clit, dreaming of being fucked on his boardroom table until she had come. He could see her in his mind naked on their sofa. Her chest and cheeks would be flushed red and her pussy glistening with juice. His cock stiffened inside the leg of his suit trousers. He knew what she liked after she had wanked was to watch him. She would giggle as his hand tugged faster and faster on his cock. When she thought he was getting close she would push out her firm breasts willing him to shoot all over them. When he did come she loved every drop that shot out. When he was spent she would gently lift his cock into her mouth and suck the last few drops from him.

He looked up into the eyes of his female colleague. He didn't know if he was blushing or if she could sense the pheromones he must be emitting, but she had a glint in her eye. She looked interested, as if she was waiting for something to happen and would not object if it did. Nothing would happen, he desired his wife far too much to consider any other woman.

"Excuse me, I have to go to the gents," he said rising from his chair and placing his hands in his pockets to hide his hard on.

In the toilet cubicle, he pulled down his trousers and boxers revealing his erect cock. He dialled his home number and as he raised the phone to his ear his other hand grasped his cock and started to move slowly.

"Hello," his wife said as she lifted the receiver.

"Hi sweetheart. I had such a hard on I had to come to the bathroom so I could wank," he told his wife.

"Have you got that lovely cock of yours in your hand right now?" she asked, knowing the answer.

"Yes and I am stroking it just for you"

The thought of him standing naked with his cock in his hand turned her on once more. She sat on the stairs and immediately started rubbing her pussy.

As they both wanked they could hear each other's breathing. No words were exchanged just sighs and moans. They knew each other so well they could tell how close the other was and adjusted their speed so that they came as nearly together as they could. He came first, the sound of his orgasm pushing her into hers.

Afterwards they both remained on the line breathing

27

deeply.

"I had better go back to my meeting," he said breathlessly.

"See you tonight," she replied and replaced the receiver.

California Dreaming
by Alison Tyler

Alden wanted to watch another man fuck me.

You just can't say it any plainer than that.

As he rolled me over in bed, parting my long legs and sliding his cock deep inside me, he whispered his favourite fantasy. "Just once," he assured me. "Oh, baby. Just one time. I know what you're like in bed. I know how you feel, and how you look, and how you taste. But I want to watch another man learn those sexy secrets. I want to see you come while he takes care of you."

"He?" I asked.

Doggy-style lets Alden go in deep, and for a moment, he couldn't respond. But even though I was as turned on as my man, I wouldn't let up, waiting only a moment before murmuring more insistently, *"He?"* as I gazed into the mirror above our bed and stared at our reflections. Alden is dark-haired and bronze-skinned, with grey-green eyes that sheen with an insatiable sexual appetite.

"You know who –" Alden said, slamming faster now, really fucking me. I slid one hand between my legs and touched my clit, fingering myself gently as Alden continued, "you *know*, baby. The pool guy."

Oh, god. The pool guy.

Alden and I rent a large, Spanish-style bungalow in

sun-drenched Santa Monica. The best part about the house is the backyard pool – a lush aqua gem in a lagoon setting. And the best part about the pool is the stunning man who comes once a week to clean it. Talk about your California dreaming ... Will is tall and long-limbed, with birch-blond hair and eyes that rival the blue of the deep end in our oval-shaped pool. Since I first saw him, I felt that naughty pang you get when you're in a long-term relationship, but you notice a particularly beautiful specimen of the opposite sex.

Although I've never been much of a swimmer, I instantly began fantasise about taking a decadent dip into the pleasurable waters of sex with Will. Now that I'd been given free reign to enjoy these fantasies, they came more and more often. In bed, in the shower, in line at the grocery store. Whenever I closed my eyes, that vision awaited me. I was California daydreaming, in a constant state of enhanced arousal. Somehow, though, the naughtiness didn't disappear even though these fantasies were greenlighted by my man. Because Alden wasn't suggesting a threesome, where he might go out and have a beer with Will at the Tapas bar around the corner, explain the sex-charged situation, then casually invite him into our boudoir – no, he wanted to watch, surreptitiously watch, while I got it on with the pool guy. And the thing of it is, nothing had ever excited me more.

"Here's the deal," I explained to my boyfriend after many pleasurable fantasy sessions. "I don't want to plan this to death. If it happens, it happens, otherwise, we can forget about it. This isn't something I'm willing to force."

That was good enough for Alden – and as it turned out, he didn't have to wait long. Next week, when Will arrived, I knew what to do. I walked by the pool in my indecently short white robe and settled myself on one of the outdoor wood-and-canvas lounges, as if I were innocently positioned there to catch a few mid-afternoon rays. Alden was upstairs in his office, and I knew that if he looked out through the blinds his window, he'd be able to see everything.

"Hey," Will said to me, quickly glancing up from his job.

"Hey," I said back, untying my white terrycloth robe and letting it fall open. I wasn't wearing anything underneath. Not a string bikini. Not a skimpy thong. With my shades on, I pretended to completely ignore Will, but I knew he wasn't able to do the same with me. No man could have. His eyes were focused on the silky expanse of skin showing in the parting of the robe. I could almost feel him grow hard from where he stood.

After a few minutes, he walked to my side of the pool, then to my side of the lounge, and finally he sat down right at the edge.

"You're going to burn," he said, reaching for the sun tan lotion.

"You mean it's going to get so hot?"

He looked at me, eyebrows raised.

"You know," I smiled, shaking the robe off completely. "When we fuck –"

That's all the encouragement he needed. But before we continued, I reached into the pocket of my robe for a condom.

"You're prepared," he grinned.

"Like you wouldn't believe."

"And what does Alden think about all this?" he asked as he rolled on the condom.

"We have an arrangement …" I whispered.

31

"Oh," he breathed, "an *arrangement*."

His hands were rich with the oil and he slid them up and down my naked body. I breathed in deep to catch the tropical scent of the oil mixed with the bougainvillea growing on the stucco and the sweet honeysuckle way at the back of the yard. I sighed and arched, and Will rolled me over and pressed me down on the towel, his shorts open, his body on mine.

I visualised Alden watching every move. I could see it in my mind as he pressed himself up to the blinds, one firm hand on his rigid cock, tugging as he watched Will enter me from behind. That thought brought me even higher as Will gripped onto my auburn ponytail and steeled me for what turned out to be a wild ride. His rock-hard body slammed into mine with each thrust. The combination of the action and the thought of my man watching everything had me slippery wet, with juices dripping down my inner thighs.

"God, you're hot," Will sighed as he bucked against me.

"On fire –" I agreed, pushing back into him, meeting and matching him stride for stride. I didn't look up to the second floor as I came. I closed my eyes and let the world disappear. Will brought his fingertips to my swollen clit, extending the pleasure for me as he drove in deep.

"Where is he?" Will hissed against my neck.

"Where?"

"Upstairs."

Will jutted his chin upward, and I felt a connection made between the three of us: me, Alden, and my new lover. Or should I say, "our" new lover?

"Tell him to come downstairs," Will demanded.

"You –" I told him, sighing. "Oh, Will, you do it."

He called out Alden's name, and then I heard the sound of feet on the steps, and the screen door opening. I looked up to see my man standing there, a waiting, willing smile on his face.

California dreaming? Maybe. But every once in a while even the most fantastic dreams can come true.

Taken
by R. Gay

I began calling her obsessively because I craved the sound of her voice.

Mostly, I would hang up once she answered, but sometimes, I lingered, breathing softly, listening to the throaty way she wrapped her mouth around, "Hello," over and over again. I pictured her tapping her long, perfectly manicured fingernails against her desk, her brow furrowing with frustration-perhaps a little fear? And then at home, she would slip out of her heels, loosen the waistband of her sensible skirt, and sink into the couch, sighing with relief, as she recounted her day to me. For whatever reason, she never told me about the phone calls. That made me wonder. I should have left well enough alone.

I'm at work, the door to my office closed. The blinds closed. I'm staring at the phone as I doodle over the day's appointments on my calendar. Then I'm dialling. The line rings once, twice. My stomach drops when I hear her voice. I am stalking my own lover.

"Hello?" There is irritation in her voice. "This is getting a little old."

I clear my throat. "Is it now?"

"About time you said something."

"You're legs are crossed right now, right over left," I

say, waving my secretary away when she opens my office door.

"My company traces every incoming call."

"Now, now," I drawl. "We're just getting acquainted."

She hangs up, and I smile, count to ten, and press redial. "What?"

"As I was saying. I bet your legs are crossed right now, right over left."

She sighs heavily, as though we've danced this dance too many times. "Yes."

"You're wearing a short, dark skirt. It crawls dangerously up your thighs when you're legs are crossed like so. You like to play it a little dangerously, don't you?"

"What makes you think I haven't called the police?" Her voice has gotten lower; it tickles my ears, among other things.

"The way you just squeezed your thighs-you're tingling in places you shouldn't." I hang up before she can answer.

At home that night, she is distracted, tense. She sits on the floor in front of the couch, her back resting against my legs. I pull her shirt down over her shoulders and rub her neck. I enjoy the way her flesh pushes and pulls beneath my hands. Leaning down, I slowly drag my tongue over the back of her neck. There are slight ridges there from years of bad posture. My hands slide forward, cupping her breasts. I lower my teeth into her skin, nibbling, my hands squeezing her breasts, pushing them upwards. She hisses, leaning further into me, her back arched at an awkward angle. Her legs cross, right over left.

"I love when you cross your legs like that," I whisper, tracing the edges of her left ear with the tip of my tongue.

35

She pulls away. "I need to shower," she says, kissing me on the forehead – a Judas kiss.

Alone, I feel heavy, nauseous. I am jealous of myself. The next morning, I lie in bed, watching her get dressed–a white cotton blouse with oversized cuffs, form-fitting black slacks, and low sling back heels-one of my favourite outfits. "Important meeting?" I ask.

She shakes her head. "I feel like looking nice today."

I don't call her for three days, but we make love on each of those three nights. We are rough with each other-I call her names, she moans for more. I take her from behind, watching the skin over her knuckles stretching as she claws the sheets. We sweat, hair sticking to our faces our bodies making wet sounds as we come together and pull apart. She looks back at me, and I get the sense that we hardly recognise each other. My fingers are folded deep inside her, where she is warm and slick and gently bruised. On the third morning, she turns over, and watches me waking up. Her lips are swollen, there is a large red mark spreading across her neck and another on her right ass cheek. The skin between her thighs is pink and chafed. She has the look of a whore and I love it.

"My, haven't you been territorial this week," she murmurs.

I drag my thumb across her lower lip. "Is that a bad thing?"

"Not at all," she says.

I drag my thumb along the column of her throat.

"Good."

I call her four hours later. "Miss me?"

"You have a lot of free time on your hands."

"I am a woman of leisure."

"I'm taken, you know."

"Taken with me," I say, confidently.

"Someone else."

"You're wearing slacks today. You're legs are uncrossed, and the muscles in your thighs are quivering at the sound of my voice."

She says nothing.

"You have long fingernails – I can hear it in your voice. Drag your fingertips along the seam of your crotch."

"Why should I?"

"Because you're taken, and it will feel so good."

She breathes faster.

"Unbutton your slacks."

"I'm at work."

"Unbutton your slacks, and slide your hand into those silk panties of yours.

Drag one fingernail back and forth over your clit. Feels good?"

"Yes," she mutters.

"Now press your two fingertips against your clit, hard, and fuck yourself, just for me. Let me hear you."

She puts on a good show, moaning as loudly as she dares, telling me in lewd detail how wide her legs are spread with her feet up on her desk and her chair against the window, how wet her cunt is, how she has three fingers inside herself, how she can't believe she's being such a whore. When she comes, her breathing is harsh. "Happy now?" she asks, angrily.

"Immensely," I whisper.

I get home from work before her, and when she arrives, slides her shoes off and sinks into the couch, I sit next to her and bring her right hand to my lips. I smell the stain on her fingers.

O Ramona
by Helena Settimana

In the end, he would protest that he did it out of love for her.

Oh Ramona, whip-cracker sharp, raven-black Ramona, with crimson lips like a comic-book thing of the night; Ramona who stole Leon's heart in her youth, which was fresh, and pure, a long time ago. Leon remembered. We're given our youth so we fall in love — sometimes almost forever.

In the indigo dark, Ramona would slither along his length, run fingers over his breadth, puff life into his veins, and he would enter her and think that nothing on earth could be so good. Ramona, bent over his wine-red velvet chesterfield, black between the legs, wine-red, too, at her core, crying when he moved in her, entreating him, calling for God, for the Devil. Leon was enslaved in his own home. It was the price he paid for love.

Ramona found Tantalus — secretive, hidden down dark, dank, foul-smelling stairs and she led Leon there, collared by his love for her. Ramona writhing in the centre of the floor, in a murder of like-clad creatures. The room was smoke and heat and the grind and bounce of bodies, sharp sweat-smelling bodies, the chemical smell of latex, the animal smell of leather and Ramona held court, Leon at her feet, if only as a metaphor. They played together – this girl and that. Slips of things they would trail over with whips and metal, trembling blades. Trembling girls. Could it be better? That was the beginning. How many years? How many loves? That was before Ramona changed, and Leon changed, prickled by a shift in his true heart's desire.

When Ramona spotted the man across the room, the one seducing her with Lucifer's eyes, she whispered in Leon's ear sand said that she must have him. She sought Leon's Grace, his blessing, so that she could have him, feel him through his second skin, feel this man move in her, too. Leon balked. Deny Ramona? Deny her? His eyes locked with the man across the room. He looked fey. That troubled Leon even more than Ramona's demand. The man raised his glass in a salute. Leon he turned to her and said:

"No."

"What do you mean, no?" she croaked in her whiskey-and-cigar corvid'svoice.

"No."

"I can't believe you said that."

"No – pick a girl."

She began to walk toward the man with the glass in his hand, her narrow hips twitching to the beat, doing her siren act.

And in that moment, Leon knew that there was one part of this drama he must enact. It was brutal – like the pulling of the trigger and the ensuing explosion when a skeet was released. It was an insane thing to do. He marched ahead of her, angrier than he'd ever been. Ramona could consume the edible girls of Tantalus, he would finish them off. But he, he, was her man. No other – not even for this. No. He pushed toward the man at the bar. At first he thought only to strike him. Then he thought to strike her. So he kissed the man, hard on the mouth. He had never done such a thing.

Leon waited to die, waited for the blow to his temple that surely would follow. He shot a steel-edged look back at Ramona, standing in the smoky haze across the room. She stopped cold, her hard, dark features compressed with surprise. The man didn't hit him – in fact, he raised an eyebrow, drained his glass and motioned Leon to follow him deeper into the club.

He didn't want her. He looked back over his shoulder, caught a glimpse of Ramona through the blue haze, and melted into the crowd.

When she found them, the look on her face was priceless – Leon feeding his hooked, hammerheaded stump into the mouth of the nameless man, tucked into a filthy corner of the alley behind the bar. The man, on his knees, pulled his own cock. Leon's face looked pained. When he finished he stalked past her spitting the words, "There's your girl. You can have her, now."

In the end, he knew he did it for himself.

High Ground
by June Sumner

I'm panting and sheened with sweat by the time I reach the top of the hill. It's never easy getting up there, but this time my heart is pounding more than usual – I know exactly what I'm going to do when I get up there.

I've been fantasising about it for years, ever since I started riding my bike up to this hill overlooking the Golden Gate Bridge. It's nice and secluded; the rocks and trees hide everything from the winding path that leads from the far end of Lake Street to the Cliff House miles away. And on a Tuesday morning, like this one, there's no one on that path anyway.

My skin-tight black spandex bicycle shorts and electric-blue jersey wick moisture away from my skin, but I still feel soaked after the long ride from the Haight. I lean my bike up against a tree and shoulder my backpack. I crawl through the rocks to the tiny promontory overlooking everything.

There, I feel like I'm on the top of the world; the bay, the city, the bridge, the Presidio, Marin County and Alcatraz are all spread out below me like the jewels in my crown. I'm the queen of the world, and I'm a very naughty queen.

I can feel my nipples hard beneath my sweat-soaked jersey; if anyone were to walk along maybe they'd just

41

think I was cold. Or maybe they'd know what I'm really here for.

I glance back; I can see my bike through the trees, so I know it's still there. Besides, I could hear anyone coming through the trees long before they got here. There won't be anyone; I feel sure of it.

I take the tattered blanket out of my backpack and spread it on the ground. There's a breeze coming up; after the hard ride it seems chilly. I sit on the blanket and fold it over while the breeze caresses my face. The blanket is perfect cover.

Under it, I squirm out of my bicycling shorts. The soft cotton blanket, washed a thousand times over the years, feels divine against my sweaty lower body. I want to squirm out of the jersey, too, to be naked here with the bridge and the bay. But I'm too nervous at first; I can't imagine being that exposed, that vulnerable.

I take out my pipe, pack it, and take one hit, then two as I look out at the bridge. That's all it takes; I'm soaring above the world, feeling the breeze through the cotton blanket touching my pussy and ruffling my pubic hair. God, I can't stand it. I'm suddenly so horny I'm going to explode. I decide I have to be naked. I pull the blanket over my head and I wriggle out of the tight spandex jersey, bunching it up deep inside the blanket. I slip my arms through the sports bra and pull it off over my head, its warm damp scent sexy to me as I let it linger on my face.

My hand finds my pussy, as wet as can be. I slide one finger in as if to reassure myself that I'm turned on; I don't really need the reassurance, though. I slip my slick finger back out and use it to circle my clit, rubbing slowly. God, that feels good. It feels better than anything I've ever felt. The euphoria of the expensive pot coursing through my naked body, I sink into the sensations as my eyes flicker from the bridge to the hills of Marin to the faraway waters of the Pacific. The sun is behind me, warm on my face even as the wind cuts through the blanket and chills me. I'm rapidly building up my own heat, though, as I mount toward orgasm, moaning softly into the wind.

I come once without using anything but my hand, just a few minutes in to my explorations. It feels incredible to succumb to the spasms of orgasm as the sky opens up above me. I'm not anything close to satisfied, though, and after I rest for a few minutes and take another small hit from my pipe, I reach in to my backpack to find my little battery-powered vibrator.

Its first touch on my clit explodes through me, and I hear myself groaning loudly. I want to stop at first, but then I realise no one can hear me. Even if they were on the path below, my sounds would be lost in the howl of the wind. I shout out "Oh, God, fuck me!" just to see what it feels like, and it feels incredible. I meet the wind with soundless moans as I slide the tip of the buzzing vibrator up and down between my swollen vaginal lips. My clit throbs underneath it and soon I'm getting ready to come a second time. I hear myself talking dirty, something I never do in real life. But now I feel set free somehow, and I say nasty things for only the wind to hear as I come closer and closer to my second orgasm. When I come, I scream at the top of my lungs, telling the Earth and the sky how fucking good it feels to fuck myself.

Now slick with sweat again, I throw the blanket off of me, and the freezing cold of the wind feels like it could strip my flesh from my bones. Now I'm naked, truly naked, and I've never felt more exposed, more delicious, sexier. I've never been more turned on than I am right now, with my legs spread and my bare pussy pointing toward Marin. Then I'm back to touching myself, my clit getting a little sore with the rubbing.

It takes me a long time to build up to a third climax, especially with the wind chilling me. But I don't want to put the blanket back over my naked body; I love being exposed here, spread out for the universe to admire. Shivering, I turn the vibrator on again and push myself toward a final orgasm. "Come on … come on …" I beg myself, and then I'm arching my back, a frigid gust of wind shooting underneath it and freezing the small of my back as I push up with my legs and lift my ass off the blanket, as an intense orgasm thrums through my naked body. Grasping my nipples and pinching, I savour the moment or orgasm at the highest point in the world – the high ground, looking down with blissful disdain on anything less pure than this. I ride on the crest of that wave for as long as I can take it, and then I sink down onto the blanket and wrap myself up in it.

I don't mean to fall asleep, naked there under the blanket with the wind crisp on my face even as the sun warms it. It just happens, and my dreams are delicious as no dreams have ever been.

When I awaken, the sun is low on the horizon and I'm shivering. I slide on my bicycling shorts and my sports bra and my jersey, then get my sweatshirt out of my backpack and put it on. Thankfully, my bike is still safe. I climb through the gap in the rocks and stop short as I see two guys, college students, coming up the path.

"Hi," one of them says, a little startled to see me. "Nice up there?"

"Out of sight," I tell him, and head down the hill

Fast Girls
by Rachel Kramer Bussel

The club is moderately crowded, appropriately befitting an average Monday night, open bar notwithstanding. Tonight, for once in a long while, I'm not interested in the free booze; I have plenty of distraction right in front of me, in the form of a lithe, little girl, who at 26 gets mistaken for 12 and is told she looks like one of the Olsen Twins. She does sometimes, but she's a chameleon, channelling a new celebrity at every turn – one minute she's Britney Spears, the next she's Elizabeth Wurtzel, and I'm not the only one who notices. Not a day goes by that someone doesn't stop and think they recognise her. She looks so sweet and innocent, and she knows it, using her simple charms for devious means. Maybe that's why I didn't know she was hitting on me the other day, even though she'd dropped numerous hints. I like that she was bold enough to just ask if she could kiss me when I didn't pick up on her hints; it's a rare girl who'll go that far out on a limb.

But that was weeks ago, before we'd become totally comfortable pawing each other all over town. Tonight we ignore my friend who's in from out of town in favour of our own corner of the couch, oblivious for the moment to the patrons sitting around us. Well, maybe not entirely oblivious. Before my eyes close as I go to kiss her, I see

a suited guy next to me, smoothly checking us out, and I
know there are others around, but I lean over and pull her
small body against mine anyway. She is such a
wonderful combination of delicate and sinful, innocent
and devious. She straddles me unexpectedly, her legs
opening over me, that mischievous smile on her face. I'm
sure that people are watching us now – I would too if I
saw us across the room.

My skirt is a respectable length, slightly above my
knee, my legs covered in thick grey tights. There's
nothing improper about it, except when I'm trying to
make out with a girl on my lap and stay relatively under
the radar. She has no such concerns, in her form-fitting
red jeans and a light t-shirt, writhing nimbly all around
me. It's like a lap dance, but much more personal. As I sit
on the couch, she straddles me with that daring smile on
her face, leaning back over the edge of the couch to show
off her flexibility. I smile too, utterly charmed by this
nymph who, despite all appearances is even bolder and
more shameless than I am. I pull her towards me,
arraying her long blond hair all around us, hoping that
makes us somewhat invisible. I'm sensing that there is
only so much farther we can go inside this club but I
don't want to leave, knowing that the magic will end if
we break the spell too early. She pushes closer to me, and
I can feel her heat through her clothes. I grab her ass and
fondle it as she leans in close to me. Her breath is hot on
my ear and I can hear tiny moans escaping from her as I
squeeze her ass cheeks, occasionally venturing lower,
seeing how far I can reach, how much I can get away
with. Each moan sends shivers up and down my body,
knowing that I can do this to her.

We're out in public, as open and viewable as possible
and yet this feels as intimate as anything we've ever

done. We don't have to care about the prying eyes because we're now in our own world, communicating on a level so intrinsic and primal that we could almost be naked right now and not even care. She presses in closer to me and I take a breath of frustration at what we can't do. She bends all the way back again, her hair falling to the floor, her yoga skills coming to life as she contorts on top of me. For one of the first times in my life, I wish I had a cock to press up against her, a concrete way to show my arousal, to taunt her with as it hit her right along her cunt. I'll have to make do with other means. I pull her face towards mine and we kiss, hot and wet and needy, her tongue diving forward to reach as much of me as she can. I bounce her on my lap and pull her even closer to me. Again, I feel like some macho guy, despite the skirt, hair and makeup, with my girl on my lap to do with as I please. I don't know that this will be the first of many nights we're told that we're causing too much of a stir, making guys' cocks hard, guys who have no clue what we do in private but like to watch the swirl of hair and lips and skin. I don't know what will happen beyond tonight, when she gets home to her girlfriend, what future we might or might not have together, and I don't care. Nothing else is as important as the way she looks sitting on top of me, both sweet and slutty. It's tricky, challenging, and a turn-on to figure out how much I can touch her here, out in the open, how many times my hand can skim over her shirt, slyly brush her nipples, how I can grab the back of her neck and squeeze it, scraping my nails lightly along that delicate skin, her heading tilting back at the contact. We keep bringing ourselves right to the edge where it almost doesn't feel worth it to stay, where we need to rip each other's clothes off as soon as possible, and then return, still on edge but manageable.

Here, in a too-cool bar where everyone is trying to out-hip everyone else, in a straight enclave in the gayest section of the city, we are too fast for the likes of those around us. We're too much – too much girl, too much passion, too unrestrained – even though we're quiet, even though we're minding our own business. Maybe they sense that underneath our long hair and public kisses, our roaming hands and blushing faces, is something more powerful than that, something that won't let us break away and sit and be quiet like everyone else. We don't care who sees us because we're not here for them, or maybe we are, partly. With her, I don't have to analyse each and every movement, calculate who is watching and who isn't, simply close my eyes as the DJ swirls Madonna all around us and take her in.

I look at her and feel so many things all at once – excitement, lust, power, hope, maybe a little bit of fear. She's unlike any other girl I've ever met, a beautiful and maybe dangerous mixture of sweetness and daring, pushing every envelope she can find. I know I like to think I'm bold, like to think I will do anything, anytime, anywhere, but this girl really will, and she wants me. She ducks her head down to my neck, then lower, peeling the already low ruffle of my velvet shirt down just a little bit more to reveal the bursting pink of my nipple. For all my wildness, I've never done anything like this before. Her hair mostly hides her face as her lips find my nipple and she licks and sucks it, light and gentle, teasing.

Maybe it's because I don't have a good poker face, never have and never will, and can't look nonchalant while this totally fast girl works her magic on me. Maybe we've just caused too much of a stir, finally worn out our lukewarm welcome. Whatever it is, I hear a knock on the wall and am too embarrassed to look up. "That's inappropriate behaviour, girls, and you're going to have to stop," says a deep male voice. I mumble something vaguely apologetic, stand up, grab my bags in a hurry. She is calm and cool and keeps talking, hugging me, not at all bothered that we're too fast for this place, too out of control. We walk out into the night and laugh, lingering, her hand on my cheek and a look on her face I don't know how to interpret. It takes us a while to say goodbye, even though the air is chilly and it's getting late. I'm not sad to go, just wistful as she smiles that mischievous smile that promises me even more trouble the next time she sees me. She bundles her long coat around her, skips off into the night.

My fast girl, I think, as I walk to my train, a smile lingering all the way home.

Handjob
by Heather Peltier

He's used to my mouth; I can't keep it off of his cock. I'm orally fixated, I'll admit. But today I've got other things in mind, as we sit cuddled up together on the couch watching movies. My hands have been wanting him all day; at lunch, I fantasised about stroking him off, and that's what I want to do.

We're leaning back against a big set of pillows, my body against his. He's wearing sweats because he was chilly; I'm wrapped in a light blanket, and stark naked underneath, as I usually am when we're relaxing around the house. My hand casually rests in between his legs, and I can just see the bulge of his soft cock through his sweat pants.

Without saying a word, without making another move or telling him that he's going to come for me, I slide it up and place it on his cock, palm open, fingers slightly curved – not quite gripping him. I feel his softness in my grasp and my heart immediately begins to quicken. It quickens more when I feel his softness start to go hard, slowly spreading and stretching against my hand, distending his light-grey sweat pants.

A shiver goes through me as I feel his cock get hard. I turn my body just enough to look into his eyes, and start stroking him up and down, through the sweat pants. He gets all the way hard in another moment, his eyes locked in mine. I bite my lip flirtatiously and slide my hand into his pants.

He's not wearing underwear. Feeling his naked, hard cock in my hand sends a thrill through me. I wrap my fingers around his shaft and start to stroke him up and down.

As if it's the most natural thing in the world, he clicks a button on the remote control, and I understand why he insisted on buying the five-disk DVD player instead of the cheaper one-disk model. He's slipped a porn movie into one of the free slots, replacing the cheesy romantic comedy we were watching with the throbbing strains of bad porn music and the faked moans of female pleasure. With my free hand I pull his sweat pants down further so I can get at his cock more completely. He glances from the TV screen to my eyes, and I get more and more turned on as I watch *him* getting turned on, the porn working its magic. Even though I don't like porn all that much, nothing gets me hotter than watching him watch porn. There's something so visceral, so intense about the way it turns him on, driving him to jerk off frenetically.

But tonight, I'm the one who's going to jerk him off.

"You like that porn, you dirty boy?" I ask him, my voice hoarse with desire for his cock. "You're so filthy to watch it with your girlfriend in the room. I bet you'd jerk off right now, if I wasn't jerking you off, wouldn't you?"

His only answer his a moan as his hips rock in time with my stroking. I squeeze his cock shaft firmly and stroke up and down, bringing my other hand around to tease his glans with my thumb while I pump his shaft. I'm incredibly wet now, feeling the moisture forming on my inner thighs as I enjoy the way his cock surges with the action on the TV screen. I move my hand down and tickle his balls, then stroke back up to his head and rub the tip, moistening his cockhead with his pre-come. There's quite a lot of it, and as I start to stroke hungrily up and down, locking my eyes in his, I see that both the porn and my eagerness are having the desired effect. He's going to come.

"Are you going to come for me? Are you going to shoot your hot come all over my hand, baby? Are you going to drench me in it?"

But I can't bear to let his hard cock go. I slow down and move my hands, loosening my grip so that I'm barely touching him, just tickling him with my palms as I twist back and forth. He squirms under me, his eyes glazed as he writhes and lifts his ass off the couch. I close just thumb and forefinger around the base of his shaft and slide it gently up and down halfway, barely touching him with the pads of my fingers, wrapping my other hand around his head and squeezing firmly and rhythmically. His head snaps back and he presses hard against the pillows, his back arching. He's grasping the back of the sofa, now, trying to steady himself as I lose all composure, consumed with hunger for his orgasm.

I grasp his cockshaft firmly with both hands and start jerking him off hungrily, desperate for his come. I pump my double-fist up and down on him, eyes fixed on his face as it twists and reddens in pleasure, his gaze never leaving me. When the first spurt explodes from the tip of his cock, I feel a rush of excitement and bring my face down to smell it, still looking at him. More come shoots out over my breasts, coats my hand and arm, even splatters on my extended tongue as I open my mouth hungrily. The whole time, he's forgotten about the porn movie; as he comes, he's staring at me as I stroke his cock.

As his cock softens, I lay my face against his chest, smelling the sharpness of his come and enjoying the way it slickens against my hand as I stroke his balls and belly. My breasts move slick against his stomach, moistened with his come.

Casually, he clicks the remote control again and our romantic comedy comes back; I feel a vague thrill at the way he just blithely took us back to what we were doing before I jerked him off.

Until the next time, that is. I know just how to get him hard again, and I think about ten minutes more of this movie is all I can stand. It won't be long, now. I can already feel his cock stirring against me.

Parking Goddess
by Xavier Acton

"Jesus, how big is this parking garage, anyway?"

The hotel where she and I had just attended a boring professional conference was twelve floors down and about a half a mile over; this parking garage was enormous. We had prayed to the Parking Goddess, and the bitch had ignored us. And so Mia had dropped me off in the hotel turnaround; I had gone in to register both of us while she parked the car.

Mia stopped, stretched languidly, her skirt tugging up over her garters. She arched her back, her small, perfect breasts eloquently distending her thin, almost see-through blouse until several of the buttons almost popped. The blouse pulled up over her belly, of which quite a bit was visible, seeing that the skirt hung low on her hips as well as making only the briefest of showings on her thighs.

She always dressed outrageously when she knew she had something boring to do. And the conference, on a software package so dull it made my eyes cross, had certainly been that. What's more, though, Mia always gets horny when she gets bored.

Mia fixed me with that mischievous look that tells me things I might not want to know.

"Uh-oh," I said.

54

Her arms snaked around me, and she pressed her lips to mine. Our tongues entwined as she pulled me hard against her – or, rather, pulled herself hard against me. I could feel her nipples, hard and horizontal through her thin blouse. If she'd been half a cup size larger she would never have been able to get away with going braless.

My arms went around her, my hands travelling to her ass and up under her skirt. She wasn't wearing much under there, just her most concise thong. I recognised it with a touch – it was the black one with little red bows, a silk-screened image of two cherries and a girly pink script that said "Juicy." Mia always wore it when she was planning on doing something really slutty. When I eased it aside and slid my hand under it, I found her wet.

"We're two floors down," she said. "But this floor is much emptier."

I pulled her skirt up and planted one hand on each of her perfect ass-cheeks, lifting her fully into the air. She's just small enough that I can do that, but I didn't want to take my chances, so I picked the nearest car, a little Japanese-made sports car. Brand new, from the lack of plates. I laid Mia down across the tiny trunk; it was just big enough for her to perch on. and she stretched out, her legs pressing obediently together as I slipped my hand under the waist of her "Juicy" cherry-flavoured thong and pulled it slowly down her thighs, over her knees, over her ankles, my eyes locked in hers the whole time. My two fingers went into her smoothly, and Mia squirmed, moaning, her thighs clamping shut around my hand. I discovered as my fingers slid into her that underwear doesn't lie. Or, at least, this one didn't, and it was as juicy as she was, soaked through. It had been a long conference, with Mia making semi-obscene doodles next to me on a hotel pad.

I tossed the thong onto the roof of the car.

"Don't forget that," she said. "It's my favourite underwear."

Mia spread her legs, her booted feet tucked onto the tiny bumpers of the sports car. I lunged forward, popping buttons on her blouse as I opened it. My mouth found her nipple and she moaned, running her fingers through my hair as I tongued her firm bud and licked my way down her belly.

She leaned back against the slanted window of the sports car, treating it like her personal chaise lounge. Her legs eased further apart as I brought my mouth between them, and when I breathed warmly on her cunt and looked up to lock her eyes, Mia appeared not to believe I was really doing this. For a moment, I was afraid she was going to tell me to stop.

So I fired a pre-emptive strike: I smiled at her.

"This was your idea, remember?" I said.

My mouth molded to her slit, my tongue licking hungrily from her moist entrance to the ringed firmness of her swollen clit. Mia slumped back against the sports car window, propping herself up on her elbows; I had to wrap my hands around her hips and push her hard against the trunk to keep her in place. She looked down at me hungrily, biting her lip to keep from moaning too loud, but as my tongue flickered down to her entrance again and let my fingers join my tongue, she couldn't stop the uncontrolled gasp that shuddered through her, her whole body twisting as I slid two fingers into her.

"Fuck," she moaned. "Right ... there ..."

I suckled on her clit, tonguing her rhythmically as I fucked her slowly with my hand, sliding my fingers deep. Her hands came to rest on my head, as if guiding me – but I didn't need any guidance. I knew the taste of her cunt and the way she reacted better than I knew anything else in the world. And I had already decided that Mia was going to come.

She was pressed hard against the hood of the car, held down by the pressure of my left arm sprawled across her belly, my left hand squeezing her breasts and pinching her nipples while I fucked her with my right. Mia began to tremble, her ass lifting off the trunk, her feet planted just firmly enough to support her as I rode her with my mouth, hand deep inside her, tongue working mercilessly. Her arms stretched over her head, searching for a handhold, wriggling helplessly as she floated in space. I could tell by the look on her face, by the way she pumped her hips against me, by the tension in her back, that she was going to come.

"Don't … stop," she gasped, and I didn't.

When she came, her ass came down hard against the trunk of the sports car, making a hollow thump. Her arms came crashing against the sheet metal, her elbows hitting so hard I thought she'd hurt herself. Then her hips began to pump wildly, ass lifted high off the car as she fucked my face, but she couldn't throw me; I kept tonguing her until she gave a huge groan of release and came down, again, the shocks of the sports car bouncing and protesting as the shrieking siren suddenly erupted from inside.

"Oh, fuck," she gasped, sliding off the sports car. "We set off the alarm."

She pulled down her skirt and held her blouse closed, and the two of us ran for the elevator. It was empty, and she buttoned up inside, giving me one last kiss.

"We left him my thong," she pouted. "My favourite one."

I shrugged. "An offering to the Parking Goddess." I

57

pressed the button for level ten.

When You Do That
by Jamie Joy Gatto

I love it when you take my hands, yeah, just like that. When you take my hands from me, and you wind a silk scarf around them. Ummmm, yes, just like that. I love it when I feel I've surrendered myself to you, my womanliness, so you can take me, yes, just like that. I love how you tell me you're hungry to eat me. I say, "Take me, I'm yours."

I love how when I look into your eyes I can see that hunger and it sparkles just below the surface. I can see that need, and it makes me blossom. I can feel myself opening up, opening tender folds of desire, wetness leaking from within. My pussy aches for you to touch it, but you don't yet. You make me wait. Instead you take my hands like you just have, apricot scarf holding them firmly together, and you kiss them. You take those same hands, and you lay me back into the cool sheets. You put my arms above my head. You rest my head upon a soft pillow.

My nipples rise as my tits are thrust out for you to see, to nibble to lick, but you don't just yet. You make me wait. And as I wait, that hunger you mentioned before, it grows in me. I am the one who wants you, your touch, your hot breath, your smooth hands. Feel me, touch my skin, my flesh, all over me. I am totally exposed. I writhe under my make-believe prison, my wisp of a scarf holds me down. I pretend I cannot move unless you tell me to, but that only makes me want to squirm. I want you. Oh, how I want you.

When you kiss my thighs I start to quiver. Oh, how do you do that? How do you make me want you, and yet not want you, to do that? It tickles, your lips so cold, so intense. I want that right there, oh, yes. Oh, no! I whimper as you near my hot pussy. I sigh as your breath covers me like a veil. Please touch me, please kiss me, please, make contact with me. I press my hips upward to meet your lips, but you pull away. You laugh a little. You say, "I know what you want." And then I start to beg you.

"Lick me, lover. Please. Take me, lover. Please." Your eyes have that fire, you are no longer playing, and with one smooth gesture, you lift me to your mouth. Plump lips take me into them. Your tongue feels like fire, like cool ice, it stings my clit. I groan, I spasm, the ecstasy from waiting is released so quickly. I love it when you do that, I really, really do.

I'd offer you the silk scarf, and I'd put my hands above my head. If only you were here, my lover, if only. I touch my own fingertips to my now ready clit. Just from thinking about you, I come. I shower a thousand rainbows from my pussy walls. I love the way you do what you do.

Stuck In Traffic
by Simon Torrio

Traffic grinds to a halt, bringing a curse to your lips. You strike the steering wheel and growl like an animal, like a pissed-off dog.

"Traffic's backed up all the way from the maze to the toll plaza," blares a sterile talk-radio voice from another car's radio, mingling with the gentle classical music you like to commute to. "It's going to be a long commute, folks."

I reach down, unbuckle my seat belt and smile at you. You give me a suspicious look; I'm radiating mischief. My eyes linger on your thighs, your businesslike grey skirt pulled up high on them. You do that when you commute because it makes it more comfortable; in any event, no one can see, right? I suspect you also do it because of the effect it has on me.

I slide my hand over and let it stray between your legs.

At first you close your thighs, giving me a dirty look. But then you seem to have second thoughts, and put the car in park, set the emergency brake. You wriggle your legs slightly apart as my fingers stroke your inner thighs.

"Go ahead," you tell me. "We're not going anywhere."

"Oh, we're going someplace," I tell you, and ease my

62

hand deeper under your skirt. When I touch your pussy it's molten, wet on my fingers. It's also bare, naked to my touch.

I would swear I see you redden. "I was wearing pantyhose," you say shyly. "I took them off."

You reach over and turn up the classical music to drown out the honking.

I politely glance around to make sure there are no trucks of high-riding SUVs in our immediate vicinity.

"Naughty, naughty," I say, and slide two fingers into you.

You're wetter deep inside than you were at your entrance. You close your thighs around my hand as you let out the E-brake and put the car in Drive. Leaning against you as the car creeps forward just a few feet, I put my lips to yours and whisper in your ear: "What were you thinking of all day? Something dirty? Incredibly dirty?"

You put the car back in Park, and the brake ratchets closed. You spread your legs further than before, planting them as far as they'll go in the seatwell. You look like you would stick one leg out the window if you could, but you have some discretion.

"What were you thinking about?" I repeat.

You answer casually, as if you were discussing business on your cell phone.

"You. I was thinking about you." The car has come to a halt, and your head tips back as I nibble at your neck where it meets your shoulder. "I was thinking about you. Fucking me. Fucking me hard."

I kiss your neck more fully, drawing my tongue around it as I let a third finger join the first two inside you. You let out a stifled little squeal and then push yourself forward in your seat, forcing your cunt harder onto my hand. I start to fuck you, pushing three fingers deep inside you and rubbing your clit with my thumb as I penetrate you rhythmically. I breathe warmly in your ear and say "What position?"

"Doggy style," you tell me. "All day I was thinking about you fucking me doggy style."

"I like doing it like that," I tell you. "I like watching your gorgeous ass as I slide into you. Plus, that way I can spank it."

"Oh, yeah," you whimper, desperately as I fingerfuck you harder. "Yeah. I was thinking about that, too. I was thinking about you spanking me as you fuck me."

I thrust deeper into you, curving my fingers with some difficulty to press against your G-spot. The car ahead of us moves and you have to fight to keep your focus on the road as you close your thighs around my hand so you can creep ahead a car length. I don't take my hand out; I force my fingers deeper into you as you drive. Then it's brake time again, the car is still and your legs are moving. Open. Spreading. Spreading far apart, as I grind my thumb hard against your clit. I work my fingers, feeling the swell of your G-spot and feeling the first hints of the contractions that tell me you're going to come. The car ahead of us pulls forward just as you cry out, your pussy clenching rhythmically around my fingers as I fuck it. You grab the steering wheel and moan "Oh, God, oh, God, oh, God –" and push yourself forward on the seat, tempting me deeper inside you.

The car behind us honks. You put your thighs together and this time I let my hand slide out from between them. You take off the brake and put the car in drive again. You creep forward one car length, two car lengths, three. Traffic is moving again. We drive through the Fast Track line and the display coaxes us forward. The meters are clear, and we pull onto the bridge moving swiftly, the wind pouring through the windows and tousling our hair. You glance over to look at me, your cheeks pink and flushed, your lipstick smeared and wet where you've bitten your lip as you came.

I put my hand to my mouth lick my fingers clean.

"Drive fast," I tell you, and you lean on the gas.

The Punishment
by N.T. Morley

Miss Pickering called Tasha into her office. When the poor girl got there, she saw that Miss Pickering's desk had been cleared off and on it was arrayed a flexible, supple cane, a large black butt-plug and a stack of pornographic magazines.

Tasha looked miserably at the ground, her face turning bright red.

"Tasha, do you recognise any of these things?" said Miss Pickering.

Tasha did recognise them – the pornographic magazines had been hidden under her mattress.

"Yes, Miss Pickering."

"Which items do you recognise? Pick them up and give them to me."

Trembling, Tasha walked over to the desk and picked up the paddle and cane, handing them to Miss Pickering.

"That's all you recognise, Tasha?"

Tasha looked up nervously.

"Yes, Miss Pickering. That's all I recognise."

Miss Pickering looked the girl up and down.

"Tasha," said Miss Pickering. "Lift your skirt and take down your panties."

Face reddening more than ever, Tasha obeyed, as she had many times before. But never with Miss Pickering.

Never here, in her office, with a bare-bottomed birching awaiting her.

She lifted her short plaid skirt and wriggled her bottom as she took her panties down her thighs and let them fall to the floor around her ankles.

"Give them to me," said Miss Pickering.

Tasha stepped out of her panties and handed them to Miss Pickering.

"What the hell are these?" asked Miss Pickering.

"Tasha, these are contraband. You were issued a G-string upon induction here –"

"It goes up my butt!" blurted Tasha.

"As a G-string is meant to," snapped Miss Pickering, raising her voice. "Tasha, from now on you will go without panties each day. Do you understand?"

"Yes, Miss Pickering," said Tasha dejectedly.

"Now lift your skirt again and show me your bottom. And spread your legs as you do it."

Tasha obeyed, leaning forward over Miss Pickering's desk as she lifted her skirt just enough to present her bare bottom to the angered schoolmarm. This placed the stack of pornographic magazines well within her gaze. She could feel the familiar heat inside her beginning as she surveyed the top magazine, one called BACK DOOR WHORES, with its naked blonde on her hands and knees, ass in the air, with garish legends promising "MAJOR BUTT ACTION!" and "SLUTS WHO WANT IT!"

Am I a slut who wants it? wondered Tasha to herself as the heat grew inside her.

Miss Pickering tsked as she ran her fingers over Tasha's naked ass. Then she reached between Tasha's legs and felt her pussy.

"Shameful," said Miss Pickering. "You'll get ten strokes. Count them."

"Yes, Miss Pickering."

Tasha's eyes filled with tears as she awaited the first blow. She had been caned before, but never by a true sadist like Miss Pickering. All the girls knew Miss Pickering was the one who would truly hurt your bottom, would make it black and blue and make you cry.

Tasha was crying already.

The first blow struck with the sizzling heat of a wildfire. Tasha squirmed and moaned "One," but did not drop her skirt. Then another blow came, and Tasha chirped "Two!" with a pained tremble to her voice. Then another, "Three!" and another, "Four, oh, oh, oh, ow, ow, ow!" each one cutting into her with fierce pain. Finally, on the fifth stroke, Tasha gasped and moaned "F–five –!" as the pain of the blow settled into her bottom; she slumped forward and threw herself across Miss Pickering's desk, her face now pressed to the porno magazines, so close she could smell the rank scent of their well-used pages, many of which were stuck together. She could also smell the sharpness of the well-serviced butt-plug, which had not been washed since the last time it was used.

Miss Pickering lifted the hem of Tasha's skirt with the end of the cane. It had fallen down when she had slumped forward over the desk.

"Tasha, if you can't keep your skirt lifted," said Miss Pickering, "then take it off."

"Miss Pickering?" gasped Tasha through her pain.

"Take it off! And spread your legs for the rest of your punishment."

Chastised, Tasha unzipped her skirt and let it fall in a plaid pool at her feet. She stepped out of it and spread her legs again, but the bottom of her blouse hung as low as her behind. Tasha knew what was coming.

"The blouse, too," said Miss Pickering. "Take off your blouse."

Tasha obeyed, looking at Miss Pickering sheepishly as she exposed her breasts to the woman's gaze.

Miss Pickering eyed the fetching fullness of Tasha's bosom. "No bra, Tasha?"

"No, Miss Pickering."

"Tsk, tsk," said Miss Pickering. "Now bend over my desk."

Tasha obeyed, leaning heavily against the desk and spreading her legs, her pert bottom now fully exposed, her face pressed hard against the pornographic magazines as she drank in their smell and that of the butt plug, also close by. Her nipples hardened against the cold wood of the desk as she prepared to be birched again.

The next blow came, and Tasha's whole body, now naked except for her Mary-Janes, twisted and writhed as she whimpered "Six." Another blow, and she moaned "Seven," her ass lifting higher in the air and wriggling back and forth as she struggled and tried not to cry out. Still another blow, and she yelped in pain, only half managing to annunciate the word "Eight!" With each blow, angry red stripes appeared on her pale bottom to complement those that were already there. When Miss Pickering landed blows nine and ten, she did it so fast that Tasha had to count them both at the same time. Just like that: whack-whack, first across one pert cheek of her bottom, then the other, in a crosswise tangle of agony as Tasha burst into tears, weeping: "Nine! Ten! Oh God oh God oh God ..."

"Tasha!" snapped Miss Pickering. "What did I tell you about taking the Lord's name in vain?"

"I'm sorry, Miss Pickering."

"Don't apologise to me," said Miss Pickering with a

sneer. "Apologise to the baby Jesus."

Tasha raised her eyes skyward, taking a deep sniff of the rank-smelling magazines before saying "I'm sorry, baby Jesus."

Miss Pickering put her hand on Tasha's bum again, running her fingers first over the angry red stripes she had just placed there, then over the faded, purpled ones – three days old, she estimated, and the more faded, yellowish ones – perhaps a week or more.

"Tasha, how did you sneak the cane into your room?"

"I slipped it into the back of my blouse and put it down my skirt, and walked very upright back to my room," said Tasha nervously.

"I assume Corrinna was involved?"

"She used it on me," said Tasha. "But I didn't use it on her."

"She's still very naughty. Tasha, you know that all punishment at this institution is to be approved by the teachers. You remember why your punishments were withheld, don't you?"

"Yes, Miss Pickering," said Tasha. "I was giggling in class."

"That's why I've prepared this stack of pornographic magazines for you. They've all been well used. You are to study each and every page of those magazines after light's-out, Tasha, *with* that butt-plug inserted. It belonged to Cassidy, but she's an advanced student; she doesn't need it any more. And you will touch yourself while you do it, Tasha, rub yourself until you come. Perhaps that will teach you not to giggle during a pornographic slideshow about the proper technique for receiving anal sex."

"Yes, Miss Pickering," said Tasha.

Miss Pickering's hand travelled up Tasha's thigh and

gently stroked her pussy, which was so moist it was sending streams of juice down her thighs. Tasha moaned and pushed herself back against Miss Pickering's hand. Miss Pickering slid two fingers in and began to fingerfuck Tasha as she clawed at the desk, sending anal porno mags scattering everywhere. Thrusts of Miss Pickering's finger struck Tasha's G-spot and brought her almost immediately to a thundering, moaning orgasm. As she came, her knees buckled and Miss Pickering had to put her arm around Tasha's waist to keep her from sliding off the desk and falling to her knees.

When Miss Pickering was done, she placed her fingers very close to Tasha's face. Tasha licked them clean obediently.

"Do you think it's acceptable for a 33-year-old woman to giggle when she's being taught how to take it in her back door?"

"No, Miss Pickering," said Tasha sheepishly. "I'm sorry."

"Your husband spent a pretty penny to send you to this program," said Miss Pickering. "I'd hate to think you weren't getting the full benefit out of it."

"Now," said Miss Pickering. "Behave in class, learn how to take it in the ass like a good little slut, and you'll get your punishment privileges returned. In the meantime, I hope today's caning has reminded you how much you want your punishment privileges back. Did that little slut Corrinna punish you as well as I did?"

"No, Miss Pickering," said Tasha.

"From the looks of those stripes on your backside, she certainly didn't. All haphazard and ill-placed. I bet she didn't even make you come afterwards."

"No, Miss Pickering," said Tasha sadly. "She didn't."

"Remember that, the next time you want to circumvent

the rules. If you've learned your lesson, you'll end up right back here getting what you want, instead of settling for that roommate of yours."

"Yes, Miss Pickering," said Tasha.

"Now get dressed. You're late for oral sex class."

"Yess, Miss Pickering," said Tasha, gathering up her clothes.

Nighthawks
by M. Christian

1 a.m. Phillies coffee house. A cup each: white and sweet for her, black for him. Nick stirred his clockwise, Darlene stirred counter.

"Chasin' the moon tonight?" Nick said, looking over at her. Her hair was the colour of fresh copper, and she wore a dress to match. Her face was lean, but not harsh, and her eyes were the green of fresh grass.

"Just watching it travel, I guess. Probably gonna be home before it sets," Darlene said smiling at him. He had a good face, with lots of character: strong chin, good nose, grey eyes hooded beneath luxurious eyebrows. Not a pretty-boy, but handsome on his own.

"Used to be able to make it myself: all the way from the silver coming up to the silver going down. No grey on the roof but I'm not a kid anymore," he said smiling at her. Under the red dress she was slim, but not skinny, breasts full and obvious even through the material.

"You don't look like you're ready to get stuck in a home to me," she said, returning the smile. He wasn't big, but he seemed to be well put together: broad shoulders, and with nothing hanging over his belt. His hands, she noticed, had character. They were like signposts to his soul: strong, elegant, with perfectly clean nails.

"You're just buttering me. Nah, just been burning too much of that midnight oil lately." He wondered about her, instantly picturing her standing in his little place: red dress tossed over a chair, silken slip floating as she walked, showing off her fine lines. He imagined a redhead's soft skin, longs legs stretching beneath the bright white slip, and the twin points of hard nipples on perfect breasts.

"Know it. Just got off a shift myself. Thought a cup might make the trip home a little easier." She wondered about his lips: strong but soft, at first a gentle graze across hers, just a mixing of breaths. Then the initial chaste one, the first touch of his to hers. Heat between them flaring with the first touch of tongues, then the roaring blaze as he tilted her head back for a longer, more penetrating kiss.

"I'm right down on Bleeker. Got a little more to do but ran out of java. Jack's place is always open." He saw himself on his bed, looking down his half-dressed body, t-shirt, shorts, socks, as she climbed up with him. The gleaming white of her slip moving just enough to give him quick snapshots of knotted, deep-brown nipples, a tight tummy, and the distant flash of curled red hairs between her long legs.

"Gotta love Jack. You work graveyard or something?" His hands. Yes, that was next: his hands. Very good hands, and she thought about how he might use them. During the kissing, when it got good, so very good, they would be on her. Not hard grabs, but rather slow grazes across her thighs, up her side, over her shoulder. Then, as the fires grew higher, a gentle rest on her skirt, a cautious knead of the hard muscles. She imagined, and could see herself spread her thighs a little, just enough.

But he'd be a good man, and wouldn't dive right in.

73

Instead, she saw him kiss her even harder, swing dancing with her tongue, and his hand rest softly on her breast. At the thought, her nipple crinkled and gently throbbed in the soft support of her bra.

"My own. I'm a hack; got one thing down but have another piece due tomorrow," he was hard and hoped she wouldn't notice – but he was also hard and hoped she would notice. She was there, live and real in his mind, smiling up at him as she reached into his boxers and pulled out his very, very hard dick. She kissed it, at first – just a soft little touch to let him know that she wasn't afraid. Then a longer, wetter, harder kiss. In his mind, he was in her mouth, with his sensitive head of his cock grazing the roof of her mouth, as he watched her bright red hair bob up and down with each in, each out.

"Maybe I've read something." She could see his chest, lightly haired with dark nipples and ridges of firm muscles. His shoulders would have a light dusting of freckles, and his arms would be thick but not burly. He would have a good manly chest. Salt, the sensation suddenly on her tongue as she sipped at her coffee. Yes, salt: she wanted – then, there – to kiss that bare chest, taste the bite of his gleaming sweat.

"Not unless you hang out in some very unlady-like places. It pays the bills, though. Where do you sling your hash?" It wasn't that she would do the things he'd seen on playing cards, in stag reels. No, that wasn't that she had his dick throbbing on his pants. It was just the thought of her being there, really there, with him in his little place. The way she smiled: he ached to see her that same smile as she stroked his dick; as she pulled off her slip to show him her lean body, her firm breasts, her dark nipples, the triangle of red curls down between her legs. He wanted all that, but all that with the smile – more than anything.

"Del Rio's down on 154th. Food's not bad and the joes don't pinch my ass that much." She wanted those strong hands to touch her, to pull her close in a tight clench. She wanted him to hold her, to squeeze her so that her body was pressed against the firmness of his chest, his tight legs, his securing arms. Then – shocking in its quick power – she wanted him in her, to fill her with his kind strength, his barely restrained power.

"Tempting, I have to say; but I'm too much the gentleman." In his mind she was turning, showing him all that she was – all that she had, a proud display of her excitement. Not shy, not hiding under the bedclothes, but smiling with pleasure. Her breasts, yes; firm, with just a little jiggle as she turned; her thighs, all good lines – a knockout; her bush, looking sweet and inviting, with her legs barely spread so he could see between; her ass, tight, strong, like a perfect pear. And – as she turned for him – always the smile, the brilliant show of red lips and white teeth. She wanted this, wanted him. That was the best part of his fantasy.

"My knight. Just as long as your pen is better than your sword." She was daring in her mind, imagining his strokes into her, his strong pounding between her tight thighs. Thinking, allowing her mind to run hot and humid, she felt herself respond. A quick blush came to her cheeks as the wetness came between her legs. The shame, though, was gone as quick as the hot, wet had come: the dance of their bodies coming together, of his member sliding into that wetness, of his breath on her neck, of his lips grazing his own, was just too damned nice.

"Don't know about that – haven't got any complaints about the sword as of yet." One playing card stuck in his mind, a favorite of his jerk-off fantasies, and her smile would go so well with it: her red, freckled body straddling him as he lay on his bed, her tits bouncing as she moved her ass up and down on his dick. He could feel her, in his mind: the way her cunt would grip him, the way her so-soft, so-wet lips would push down and pull up with each wild bounce. Smiling, of course, as she fucked herself on his very hard dick.

She felt a new flush, a kind of fear: too much, too much. Good, damned yes, but it was too much: she wanted to touch him, to run a hand across his cheek, to feel the muscles there, the slight sandpaper of his almost-invisible shadow. She wanted to say something, to bring it about. No — no, it was too scary, too present. "This late I don't know if anyone would be able to find anything," she said.

He felt a heaviness. She was still there, fucking herself on his so-hard dick, but part of himself felt the illusion fall. If she came with him she probably wouldn't smile, probably wouldn't show him her body with pride and excitement. Maybe a handjob, maybe just a promise for sometime later that would never come. "I know. Except maybe the moon. Shouldn't stop us from trying though," he said.

"Always willing to try — but, you know, I think it's going down," she said, a little bloom springing up. Maybe, maybe, maybe. She touched that hope, and kept smiling at him.

"Happens to all of us. Long nights, too little sleep ... you know," he thought. But, he thought, she just might. The illusion flickered but didn't die — he held it, looking at her pretty face, and smiled back. Maybe —

"Too well. Sometimes I think the only thing that keeps me going is the joe," she said. She held it, the dream of him kissing her, of his broad chest, his strong thrusts, the chills and wonderful shivers of him inside her. Not tonight – no, but there's always the next day.

"Good dreams. See you in here tomorrow?" he said, trying to keep the quaver out of his voice, the precious grip on his dream from slipping. It was a good illusion: so real and … too complete not to give it a try.

"It's a date – I'll just follow the moon," she said, swallowing back an octave of pleasure. Not today, but maybe later – maybe sometime soon, maybe even tomorrow.

"See ya," he said as she got off the stool and picked up her handbag.

"Bye," she said as she passed him and walked towards the glass doors.

He watched her go, and smiled –

At the doors she looked back, and returned it.

Oiled For Pleasure
by Sage Vivant

"I see someone's had a lot of sun this summer," Francesca observed as her hands glided over the smooth contours of Natalie's firm ass cheeks.

Was she referring to her tan lines or her summer-bleached hair? The woman made her nervous, always remarking on things that felt too personal to Natalie.

"Yes, lots of sun," Natalie said into the terrycloth-covered donut around her face. She was glad not to have to look at Francesca – she'd be better able to relax, which was, after all, the point of the massage.

"I'll bet you look great in your bikini," the masseuse continued.

"My boyfriend thinks so," Natalie replied, hoping that the reference to David might cool the woman off.

Francesca's palms slid up her thighs and danced dangerously close to the gap between her legs. "Mmmm," she said, concentrating on the flesh beneath her hands. "I'll bet he does. You look great even without the bikini."

"Thank you." She made a silent vow to find a new masseuse. This one tied her muscles up in knots.

Starting at the small of her back, Francesca pressed the balls of her palms into the graceful slope and pushed her way up along either side of Natalie's spine. The movement was slow, deliberate, penetrating. By the time she reached her shoulders, she'd squeezed a groan out of Natalie's throat that surprised them both.

"I think you needed that," Francesca commented.

Natalie gasped, as much out of humiliation as physical relief. The woman had released something, there was no denying that, but then, wasn't that her job?

"I've been pretty tense. I seem to carry stress in my back and shoulders."

"Everybody does, honey. Leave your sexy body to me and I'll make sure there's not an ounce of stress left in you by the time you leave."

Natalie had been coming to Francesca for several months. She admired what the masseuse could do with her hands and each time she arrived for an appointment, she promised herself she'd concentrate on surrendering to those hands. Everybody else seemed to be able to do that quite easily. Then again, everybody else had a different masseuse.

"Do you like this oil?" Francesca asked. Her fingers worked the *latissimus dorsi* expertly.

The oil. Yes, it was nice. Something about it was familiar, even though it was different from what Francesca normally used.

"Yes, it's pretty. What is it?"

"It's a special blend. I call it Femme."

"What's in it?"

"Don't laugh, but a client gave it to me. She said that in addition to lavender and hyacinth, it contains the same essential oils that are in a woman's sexual juices."

Natalie's cunt tightened and then pulsed several times in succession. She didn't want to be talking about sexual juices with this woman. She especially didn't want to be excited by talking about them.

"I don't know if I'd want to work at *that* factory," she joked.

Francesca's throaty laugh filled the small room. "Now that's a delicious image. I may have to masturbate to that one."

"Francesca, I don't think —"

"Please. Call me Fran."

"Fran, I don't think this is the kind of conversation we should be having. I just want a massage."

"I'm sorry, sweetheart. Aren't I giving you a good massage?"

Her fingers were suddenly between Natalie's legs. Natalie couldn't discern how much of her slippery pussy came from the oil and how much was her own wetness. Moving meant showing her breasts to Fran, so she stayed put, trying to keep her legs together.

"Fran, really, you should probably stop."

"You said you wanted stress relief. I get the sense you're carrying a lot of tension between your legs."

"No, really. I don't think so. My boyfriend takes care of that part of me." She desperately hoped that another mention of David might do the trick. To her complete dismay, her juices were spreading to her thighs. She was creaming into Fran's hand.

"Do you get this wet for your boyfriend?" Though it was somewhat playful, the slap that landed on her ass conveyed very little nonsense. It didn't hurt but even Natalie understood that it wasn't supposed to induce pain — it was intended only to announce the larger woman's power over her.

With her other hand, she spread more oil all over Natalie's well-toned ass. "You know, sweetheart, every time you come here, I rub oil into your pretty little tush and I think about what you must taste like. I think it's about time you satisfied my curiosity." She slapped her again. "Roll over."

She gently but firmly placed a strong hand on her client's hip, then guided Natalie's body to its side and finally its front. Natalie had no choice but to follow the woman's unspoken instruction. Before she knew what had happened, she was supine, exposing her naked front to Fran.

"Oh, yes," the masseuse purred. Her dark eyes glowed darker and she seemed taller, even wider, than usual. Her gaze travelled the length of Natalie's waiting body, lingering on her breasts.

She traced the tan lines across Natalie's breasts with a unexpected tenderness. "I don't know what's hotter; seeing you naked or imagining what you look like in a bikini."

But then the tenderness morphed into something more feral. She filled her hands with Natalie's breasts and squeezed, massaging them as if they were uncooperative muscles.

"Beautiful fucking tits," she said in a voice much lower than she'd ever used before.

Natalie felt certain she was dripping onto the massage table.

"I can smell your pussy," Fran said through a wry grin. "You think if you clamp your thighs shut, I won't know that you want me to play with you. Isn't that why you shaved for me?"

"I didn't shave for you!"

"I love smoothly shaved pussies," she growled. One hand slid down her torso until it danced at her hairless muff. "I like to see my food before I eat it."

"No, Fran. Stop." Natalie protested, instinctively spreading her legs.

Fran's fingers worked their way into Natalie's slick folds. She knew exactly where to touch her, riveting her to the table, making her cunt ache and spasm like nobody ever had before. She stared down at her client as a master stares down a dog to show it who's boss. Natalie dared not even whimper.

When she'd whipped Natalie's pussy to a froth, she climbed up onto the table. Her long, substantial legs were stockingless under her white medical coat, and as she hoisted herself onto the table, Natalie noticed that she wore no underwear. Her dark pussy hair was peppered with grey but nicely trimmed. She tried not to look at it for very long, but Fran caught her and just laughed in that self-congratulatory way she had.

She knelt on the table, settling between Natalie's spread-eagled legs. Without warning, she took hold of her client's ankles and pulled upward, sending Natalie's oiled body downward toward Fran. Her legs were now perpendicular to the table and sticking up in the air. Her wide-open pussy, fragrant with excitement, hovered at Fran's chin. Fran still held Natalie's ankles, keeping them arms length apart as she surveyed the succulent feast before her.

''Look at that luscious cunt.''

Natalie was mortified by her own arousal. Did this mean she was a lesbian? All she wanted at this moment was Fran's mouth on her snatch. What was taking her so long?

Fran stared a bit longer. ''You're actually getter wetter by the second, you little slut. I'd like to make you beg but we've only got a few minutes left.''

Her tongue moved like a rubber spatula around Natalie's wet crevices. It wiggled and squirmed with a mind of its own, but a mind that anticipated Natalie's most carnal, basic desires. It stroked and massaged like a tiny pair of hands.

What Fran's tongue did to Natalie's throbbing clit defied definition. It frigged her faster than a finger, sending her into paroxysms of pleasure. When she exploded into Fran's juice-smeared face, the woman refused to stop eating her – the initial discomfort and pain eventually careened into another round of orgasmic release. Fran stopped when she sensed Natalie was close to losing consciousness.

Natalie was vaguely aware of noises and movement as she regained her faculties but didn't have the strength to open her eyes to take visual note of their source. Fran had released her legs and disembarked from the table. Beyond that, Natalie was lost in a swirling world of sensory echoes.

When she felt Fran get back on the table, though, she forced herself to open her eyes. What greeted her was the 48-year-old masseuse, her big firm tits topless, nipples erect, and a hopelessly thick black dildo hanging from a harness around her hips. Her dark skin glistened with oil, giving her the appearance of an undulating snake.

"You need to be fucked, young lady. That's the final step in stress reduction."

She fucked with male precision, slamming into Natalie's cunt with the perfect force and rhythm. Still recovering from her earlier orgasms, Natalie was especially vulnerable to the woman's thrusts, and came in a series of loud yelps as she gripped the sides of the massage table. Though she'd never confess it, the sight of Fran's bouncing tits as she rammed her would be an image she would masturbate to for many months.

When Natalie came to, Fran was standing by her side, looking down at her with benevolent sweetness. She wore her white coat again and there was no sign of the dildo. The scent of the oil and Natalie's pussy still permeated the room, however.

"Feeling better?" Fran asked, massaging Natalie's breasts with a small amount of oil.

"Yes. Yes, I am," Natalie couldn't fight the grin that spread across her face.

"Well, get up and send in my next client, would you? Leave your check on the table on your way out."

The Interview
by Lesly Sloan

When Marge Kantor at the Graduate Centre invited me to attend a reception for Nancy Chu, I was thrilled.

"Sharon," she said, "I know how hard you've been trying to sell pieces to newspapers and magazines. It's tough for an aspiring writer to get her foot in the door. I've known Nancy for a long time, even before she became famous. She was one of my brightest students but who would have thought she'd write a best-seller about her life as a call girl? I'll ask her to give you an interview, one you can use for an article."

I was grateful for Marge's offer and secretly excited by it. Not only was I having trouble placing my work, but my love life had evaporated. Tommy left town for a better job, so I was horny, as well as unsuccessful in my chosen field. I really wanted that damn interview.

The day of the reception I was nervous as hell. In the mirror I saw a cute and shapely college girl, but not an accomplished writer. 'No way Nancy will be impressed', I thought. "Fuck it – I'll do the damn interview anyway."

Nancy caused quite a stir when she arrived. She was taller than I'd expected, dressed in an outfit that showed off her curves and long legs. Rather than matching my image of a whore, she was a beautiful upscale woman, one I could easily imagine on the arm of a wealthy man.

After she'd been in the room for a while, I saw Marge go over and talk to her. At one point in their conversation, Marge pointed to me. I felt stupid and wished I hadn't come. Why the hell would she want to talk to a kid like me?

Finally, Marge led Nancy over to where I was standing and introduced me as one of her rising stars. Then Marge stepped away and left us alone.

Nancy obviously knew how embarrassed I felt and was kind enough to ask me how the writing career was going.

"Not too well," I replied. "It's hard to start out as a writer. There are lots of beginners out there, all trying to get a break."

She laughed. "Tell me about it. The only way I could sell stuff was when I submitted material about my life as a call girl. Before that, my submissions went into a wastebasket, I'm sure."

"Can I ask you personal questions?"

"Of course. I was explicit in my biography and I've been on TV, talking about providing sex for money. Well ... Maybe not very explicit."

"What does that mean?"

"I don't use the word 'fuck' in interviews and don't discuss my cunt. I talk about 'making love', and how different clients behave during sex. That's titillating enough for public consumption. I mention blow jobs in my novel, but not in live interviews. The networks don't permit such language. They're afraid of losing their licenses."

She glanced at her wristwatch, saying, "Sorry ... I'm on a tight schedule. Ask your questions."

I was staring at her cleavage. She exuded sex. Then our eyes met — she knew exactly how excited I was getting, the bitch! Maybe she had a sixth sense when it come to sex. Was she always like that, or had she developed it over time? Maybe it was a good question for the interview, but I wanted to cover other things first.

"Your current clients – are you still a call girl, or have you moved on to other things?"

She smiled, "Do you think I'm too old to attract men?"

My face flamed, "I..I didn't mean that. You're a beautiful woman. But, after making so much money doing stuff like a book and TV interviews, do you have to fuck guys for money?"

Right after I said that, I wondered if she would be pissed off at the question. But she answered with no hesitation, "My dear, I don't fuck just for money. I never did. But, generally speaking, men of power and means are more interesting than the average guy on the street. And money is important, don't you agree?"

Now she seemed to be interviewing me. How did she do that?

"I think money is important, but not the most important thing."

That sounded stupid, even to me. But she'd put me off my plan. What the hell else had I meant to ask? Nancy looked at her watch again. It was time to continue, or else I had to walk away with not enough for an article.

The question came out of my depths, not planned in any way.

"Have you ever done women?"

She looked more closely at me, as if she saw how wet I was.

"Are you asking me if I service women? If I lick their cunts until they squeal and squirm, if can I capture a clit between my teeth and tease it with my tongue until it

87

throbs like a cock? Yes, I've done women, some famous ones you've heard of, and others who aren't famous. They are quite rich and pay well. From time to time, I still take women, if they please me. You mustn't use that in your interview. If you do, I'll have your head. Understand?"

I was stunned by her vehemence and passion, more than I'd expected in an interview. She was a hot woman, like no other I'd ever met!

"Yes, I understand. What you just said about other women won't be in my article ... but I want to ask you a related question, if I may?"

"What?"

"How much do you charge your female clients?" As I said that, I blushed again. Was I out of my fucking mind? After a long pause, Nancy smiled and said, "I'm much too expensive for you. Too bad, I find you attractive, and I think you're capable of giving me what I want in return. I like to have a woman eat my pussy, run her lips over my thighs, suck on my nipples, all sorts of things. It would be a marvellous experience for *both* of us."

I was stunned at her statement, suddenly swimming between my legs.

Not knowing what else to say, I blurted, "I don't have much money; I'm just starting out."

Marge approached and told us it was time to terminate the interview, that I'd taken enough of our honoured guest's time.

Nancy gave me a long look, dark eyes travelling the length of my body. Then she reached into her purse, wrote something on a card, and handed it to me, "This is my private number. Call me, I'll work out a scholarship for you."

Lunch Break
by Shelly Baer

She couldn't stop thinking about him and each time she did her pussy tingled. She thought of his hands caressing her neck and back, working their way down to grab hold of her ass. She thought of his lips touching hers and she couldn't help but wonder what their next meeting would be like.

Despite her best efforts at keeping her mind on her work she couldn't resist the temptation to slip into the extra office when everyone was at lunch. She locked the door, sat down and raised her skirt. Slipping her hands into her panties she quickly found her hot, swollen clit. She was so turned on by the direction her thoughts had taken all day that she could barely control herself at the slightest touch.

She put her feet up on the desk in front of her, spread her legs wide, leaned her head back, closed her eyes and gently let her fingers work over her clit:

The picture in her mind was very clear. The office was deserted and she was working late, she was tired and a little cranky. Her mind kept wandering to him and her frustration that she had to cancel their date to work threatened to overwhelm her, so she pushed it from her mind and kept working. Finally she was able to kick into overdrive and was really making progress when she suddenly felt like she was being watched. She turned to see him standing there, holding a single red rose and smiling at her. She jumped up to welcome him, saying how happy she was to see him. He didn't respond, just leaned down to kiss her. She lost herself in his lips and mouth. Closing her eyes and savouring the feel of his body pressed up to hers, his strong arms holding her and his knowing hands caressing her back.

He manoeuvred her against the desk as they kissed. For a fleeting moment she wondered if he was going to do what she thought he was, but just as quickly the thought fled, because she really didn't care, she just wanted him. While she was thinking he was kissing, he kissed her face, her neck, her ears and finally worked her way down to her breasts. Never bothering to remove her blouse or bra, he just teased her through the soft thin fabric of her blouse. In a million years she would never have guessed how this kind of torture would affect her. Her body was on fire. Her hips were grinding into him without her even realising she was moving.

He gently pushed her back so that she was lying on the desk and he was sitting in the chair. With great care he spread her legs and removed her panties, slowly pulling them down her legs and then stuffing them into the pocket of his jacket. She just watched him, her eyes half open, she was mesmerised by the intensity of his stare and the deliberate movements he was making. She could feel the moisture in her pussy, she could smell her excitement in the room, she was trembling with desire. Slowly he lowered his head to her throbbing pussy. Her eyes slid closed and her hips jerked at the first flick of his tongue.

Very slowly at first he teased her clit, moving his tongue in slow gentle circles, applying just enough pressure to make her feel it but not enough to take her where she so desperately wanted to go. As she started to whimper with her need he increased the pace of his tongue sending it flicking over her hot clit and swishing it around her pussy. She grabbed his hair and pressed her pussy into his face. He inserted first one, then two fingers deep into her core and started fucking her while his tongue worked its magic on her clit.

Her breath was coming in quick and shallow gasps as she neared her peek, he sensed how close she was and abruptly stood up and released his throbbing cock from the confines of his pants and with no hesitation thrust right into her. Grabbing onto her hips he slammed into her with all the passion that was coursing through them both. It didn't take long for him to reach his peek listening to her moan and tell him to fuck her harder. Just as she was silently screaming her release he thrust into her with all his strength and let himself go.

As her fantasy characters reached their orgasms she could feel her own orgasm building. Her muscles were tightening from her toes to her shoulders, the familiar tingling in her stomach was increasing. The fingers on her right hand were flying over her clit while her left hand was caressing her breast, her breathing was rapid as she let out a silent scream, much as her character had done and squirmed and twisted in the chair with the intensity of her orgasm.

Slowly she calmed down, feeling very relaxed. She stood up, adjusted her clothes and walked out of the room.

Well, that was a nice little lunch, she thought, *I wonder what he's up to ...*

The Mirror
by Sabrina Ingram

I noticed him as soon as he stepped into the dingy pub. Faded jeans, a tight white T-shirt and a leather jacket hugged his lean muscles and my eyes were drawn past his broad chest and flat stomach to the impressive package beneath his belt buckle. The shaggy cut of his black hair and rough stubble on his firm jaw line gave his good looks that dangerous air most women, including myself, find so irresistible.

His eyes scanned the room as he walked towards the bar. He stopped next to the stool I occupied at the bar and ordered a beer from the pretty bartender ignoring her obvious look of invitation as she opened it. He took the beer and turned to me.

"What's a good girl like you doing in place like this?" he asked with a blend of mischief and desire in his dark eyes. My previous anger and frustration began to recede, replaced by a surge of lust.

"Thinking about what an asshole my boyfriend is," I answered honestly.

A dark brow quirked inquiringly.

Needing no further encouragement I unloaded all my pent up anger on him. How I'd been on my way home from a very important business trip that had kept me away for three weeks, only to have my car break down.

To make matters worse, when I called to tell Jamie that I would have to spend the night in this two-bit town on the side of the highway while it got repaired, he'd picked a fight with me. He'd planned a romantic evening in anticipation of my return, even cooking dinner, and was mad because his surprise was ruined. When I suggested he drive the hour to come and spend the night in the motel with me, like a little boy sulking, he hung up on me!

"So I've been sitting here for two hours, alone, bored, and frustrated." I finished. "Very frustrated."

"I have something that'll make you feel 100% better." he said and shifted closer.

"Yeah," I asked flirtatiously. "What would that be?"

He leaned in so that his warm lips brushed my earlobe as he whispered "Me." The heat from the hand he placed meaningfully on my stocking clad thigh spread rapidly through my body.

A shiver ran down my spine as my mind went blank. "YES!" My body screamed. "Let's go." my lips answered.

We quickly crossed the street to the old motel where I already had a room. My fingers trembled with excitement at what was about to happen, causing me to fumble a little with the key in the lock. We stepped inside and I looked around the room. It looked and smelled clean, but it was obviously a cheap motel room. Perfect for a secret rendezvous.

I set my purse down on the dresser by the wall and turned to look at him. I slid the jacket of my business suit slowly down my shoulders and dropped it to the floor, revealing the skimpy camisole beneath. I could tell by the look in his dark eyes as he stepped towards me that we both wanted the same thing. A hot sweaty session of love'n that would last all night. He stopped in front of me and gently cupped my head bringing his lips to mine in a slow seductive kiss. A kiss that quickly changed to hot and hungry as our tongues tangled. I felt his cock harden against me and his hands slid into my hair. He gripped a handful of hair and pulled my mouth from his.

"Not so fast."

He smiled devilishly and turned my body to face the mirror over the dresser. Stripping off his own jacket, he stepped behind me. Pressing his sculpted chest against my back and his hard package against my ass, he made eye contact with me. Watching my eyes he then lowered the straps of my camisole over my shoulders towards my waist, momentarily hooking the lace edge on my stiff nipples.

"Look at yourself," he whispered "how hard your nipples are, begging for attention. Your eyes are begging too. Don't worry, I'm going to give you what you want. What you need."

His hand cupped my breasts from behind, tweaking my nipples, pinching and rolling them causing me to gasp sharply. The sight of his hands on my pale skin made all the sensations rippling my insides that much stronger. My breath began to come in pants as his hands worked my body and his lips began to nip playfully on along my shoulder and neck. My hands reached behind and grabbed the firm cheeks of his ass, pulling him against me harder as I shuffled my feet further apart.

"Oooh poor baby," he crooned in response to my urgings. "Things moving too slow for you?"

His hand slid down my soft belly skin to the front of my skirt, pressing against my pubic bone. Teasingly his fingers began a walking motion that brushed my skin lightly at the same time as raising my skirt. When only my panties covered my pubes he scraped his fingers along my crease and laughed softly. "You're almost ready for me."

I whimpered and he pressed his fingers against me more firmly. My hips swayed encouragingly. His hand left me briefly and with a quick jerk elastic snapped and my panties were gone.

The image framed in the mirror was so hot. The reflection showed me standing with both my camisole and skirt wrapped around my waist, black garter and stockings framing my pouting pussy. His firm tanned arms surrounding me, his eyes burning brightly as he watched his hands glide over my body. Me soft- him hard, me light- him dark, a study of contrasts.

Another groan escaped as I watched his hand reach my pussy lips only to spread them apart, causing my aching swollen clit to thrust out rudely. His other hand hovered over my aching button, index finger pointing.

"Please …" The word trembled off my lips, my eyes searching his in the mirror. He brought his finger up to his mouth, his lips parted and his pink tongue darted to wet the tip teasingly. Our eyes met as he lowered his finger again, this time stopping directly on my clit, and with firm circular pressure I was off.

One touch was all it took to make my eyes slide shut and the fireworks to start. My knees buckled, my head rolled back, and my juices flooded his fingers and my thighs. His body stayed pressed to mine the whole time, keeping me standing. When I came back from the fireworks show I was wrapped tight in strong arms and held against a hot, hard, very male body.

"OK?" he asked softly.

"Yes," I purred.

"Good." He pressed his hips against me firmly. "Now

we can get to it."

Those words made my body hum in anticipation of more pleasure. I tried to turn to him but he grabbed my hands and placed them firmly on the dresser commanding me to keep them there.

The posture thrust my butt out and made me feel both naughty and hot. I watched in the mirror as he stepped back to rid himself of his clothes. When he was naked I could see his throbbing cock straining towards me making my mouth water.

"Later." He stated, reading my desire in the licking of my lips. "Right now I am going to fuck you so hard you'll be lucky if you can walk tomorrow."

I just spread my legs further apart and arched my back in invitation. Showing him where to put that cock of his and daring him to do as he promised.

"Ohh," he groaned. "You've got a fantastic ass, baby."

Grabbing both cheeks in his hands he squeezed and massaged them before he bent over and took a sharp nip. One hand left my ass and he dipped a finger into my wet hole. Teasing me a little more, he added another finger when my hips began to match the rhythm of his strokes.

"Oh yeah, your cunt is so hot and tight. My fingers aren't enough though are they? You want me to fill you up don't you?" He asked in a harsh whisper.

He pulled his fingers out, one hand grabbed my hip and the other guided his cock between my spread legs. Poised at my entrance, both hands grasped my hips firmly, and with one quick hard thrust he filled me completely.

My head fell forward as he closed his eyes and started to thrust in and out. His cock was hot and thick inside me; every move he made caused fantastic friction. Every few strokes he'd swivel his hips sharply, thrusting even deeper, hitting a hidden pleasure point buried deep within me. My panting shifted to whimpers of pleasure as he picked up speed. Soon his fierce pumping caused my hands to slide from the edge of the dresser to the wall behind it, giving me leverage to push back.

"Oh yeah," he growled. "That's it."

He leaned forward enough so he could grab a swinging breast. Palming it roughly he pinched my nipple and felt the answering clench of my pussy walls around his cock. I could feel my insides coiling tighter as he did it again and again. His hand then left my tit to grab a handful of my hair and pull my head up so our eyes met in the mirror. I saw sweat beading on his forehead and lips stretched taut across his teeth and I knew he was holding back. Waiting for me.

"Yes, yes, that's it. There. Harder." I cried out as my cunt clenched and another orgasm hit me. My insides began milking him, our eyes never separating. I saw sparks go off in his when he clenched his teeth, a final groan escaping his lips as his cum shot into me hotly.

My head fell forward onto the dresser and I struggled to stay standing in the aftermath. Strong arms pulled me up and snuggled me into a warm hug. Soft kisses were placed on my neck and a voice whispered in my ear. "I wasn't sulking when I hung up on you. I just wanted to get to you as soon as possible."

Butch Hands
by Sharon Wachsler

I notice women's hands. Butch hands. I know a pair of talented hands when I see one. Butch hands with grease stains or dirt smears. Butch hands smelling of parsley or red wine. Butch hands toughened and cracked with arthritis. Butch hands smooth and soft and still learning they *are* butch hands.

I keep an eye on women's hands. Butch hands. Big, muscular hands with flat, blunt fingers are good. When those hands grab you, you're not getting away. When those hands sail down, reverberate against your ass, they tattoo red reminders. Those hands own you. Under those hands you stay slapped.

When a finger on such a hand slides inside you, you feel full, engorged. And the more it surges in, the more power you hold, taking in those tough fingers, those immense hands. Devouring them, you cry, "More, more, more."

I watch for dyke hands. Butch hands. Small, nimble, delicate hands are good. One of those hands can slip behind your back and unhook your bra from outside your blouse. When you turn around, startled, feeling your breasts suddenly fall loose, open, waiting, those hands can steal up under your slip, cup your breasts in the sudden cool of a palm, squeeze your nipple between forefinger and middle finger. Make you gasp.

Tan, quiet hands with silver rings on all four fingers are good. Heavy, thick, carved rings, that make you want to lower your head to them like an animal bending to drink from a stream. Make you want to look up through your lashes, implore, "May I?" and lift the hand gently, cradle it. You start with the index finger, licking the tip, lightly tonguing the pearl of nail, the fingerprints, reading her identity with your tongue. Then suck it inside, fast, bumping up against that silver ring, that hard, hard ring against your soft lips. Opening your throat you taste its metal tang, the blending taste of flesh with something colder, more basic. The sensation reminds you of your labia bumping against the ring at the base of the harness that holds the cock in place. "Here is the limit," it taunts, "you can't go any further." Yet you try to swallow it all.

You close your mouth around one jewelled finger, moving it in and out, your teeth, lips, tongue, doing all the work, holding the hand still in your own warm hands, letting the butch feel you work, devoting your whole being to this one finger, her finger, a butch finger. Sometimes sucking hard and fast, sometimes slow and light, opening your throat, taking in the hand as deeply as you can. You would swallow her arm if you could, and she knows it.

Quick, flashing magician hands with agile wrists are good. They can confuse and bewitch you, drive you mad. Stroking feather-light, almost imperceptibly, against your clit – it feels so good that you can't understand it. It is unutterable. You thrust your hips toward that one, small stroking finger, but it anticipates, moves away before you make contact, then lays quietly on your thigh as you try not to thrash, to moan, to beg. This mean little finger, this butch finger; this kind, smart finger appears over your

99

clit again, not touching it so much as moving the air around it, letting the breeze suck your clit.

"Please," you moan, reaching over to grab the hand, but before you can make contact it has entered you, this one small finger, dazzling your cunt with its speed and talent. You cry out. Then, just as quickly it is gone. Disoriented, devastated, you look around, and that is when they pinch you – sharp little fingers biting into your thigh. You intend to scream but now two fingers have entered you, two bony, insistent fingers, then three, then four, sliding in and out, savvy fingers curved up to strum your g-spot, like waves lapping against your clit, and there: the master trickster is the thumb, gliding across your clit, with each thrust of the hand.

It is the best sensation possible. Hot blood surges to your toes, to your finger tips, to your cunt. It feels so good you never want it to end. It feels so good you can't bear it and need to come. "I need to come, I need to come, I need to come," you slur. "Fuck me. Make me come."

And then the other hand is on your ass, is cupping your cheeks, warm and grainy. Then the hand is slapping your ass, your inner thighs, and you are screaming, opening your legs wide to let more of that hand in, to take that butch hand in as far as you can.

And still, the first hand, the small, nimble, magic hand, is fucking you, in and out, thrumming your clit. And you feel something beneath you and then the second hand is there, wet with lube, a finger tracing your asshole. Around and around, teasing you, opening you; you groan and thrust toward it, but the fingers are fast and move away. Suddenly all is silent and still – her fingers inside you, her other hand laying spread on your ass. And you hear her breath and your breath, feeling your cunt jumping against her hand, in this torturous stillness. You want the hands to move again, both of them. You have never wanted anything so bad. And just as you say, "please," both hands are inside you, four fingers sliding in and out of your cunt, one finger sliding in and out of your ass. You can feel them both rubbing against each other, your clit hungry, everything wet and moving and full of friction.

And then her mouth is on yours, her tongue deep, reaching for your throat. And that is when you come, screaming into the butch, hot waves crashing against your clit, your cunt releasing like a dove bursting into flight from a magician's hand. Those hands are wet and tired and red. They are sticky and smell like you. You lick them like a deer cleaning its fawn, sucking your juice off each finger, examining it; each nail, each joint, each ridge, each scar knows you, has been inside you, has carried you towards flight.

He Just Fucks
by Jocelyn Bringas

His ice-cold blue eyes burned into my flesh, as he gazed at me. There was no expression on his face which made me feel small, vulnerable, uncomfortable, nervous, and excited all at the same time. I wanted to know what he was thinking and feeling. Was he happy to see me or was he angry at my presence? I suddenly wanted to disappear into thin air, wishing I hadn't listened to the nagging voice in my mind.

My heart pounded in my chest and I wondered if he could hear it. I desperately wanted to touch him, to feel his soft skin beneath my fingertips. I just wished my courage would take over me so I could just get this over with and fulfil my craving. I knew he was bad. He was one of those assholes that just fucked girls for fun, no love, no commitment involved. I didn't care though, I needed him.

"Are you just going to stand there and stare at me like I'm some sort of fucking statue?" he said snidely which shattered the silence between us. Hearing him speak threw my guard off and I felt myself shaking in my shoes.

"I'm sorry," I said softly. I barely heard myself and mentally slapped myself for coming off as wimpy.

"You couldn't stay away right? That's why you're

here? Your pussy is dying for my cock isn't it?"

I felt his hand sink into my arm, pulling me inside his mansion. He was a rich prominent man who probably had enough money to buy countries. Maybe that was part of his appeal.

After shutting the door, he shoved me against it. I looked up at him, my heart racing with anticipation. My body was on fire and I just wanted him to touch me all over. He took a few steps back and tilted his head to the right.

"Take off your shirt," he commanded and I wanted to cry right there.

I didn't want to go through this teasing torture, I wanted to get right to the point and get to the sex. I was afraid to protest though, in fear he might throw me out and I would be left without my fix.

As I reached for the bottom of my shirt, my hands trembled as though I was standing in the middle of Antarctica.

"I don't have all day," he complained.

I quickly removed the shirt, leaving me there in my bra, panties, miniskirt, and heels. His face was still emotionless as he stepped forward and leaned into me. I could feel his breath brush my face and he just looked at me. I shuddered when I felt his large hand run down my arm, and then to the valley between my thighs. I gasped feeling his palm through my panties. Closing my eyes, I felt him rub my soaking pussy.

"Like that, baby?" he asked whispering into my ear.

I couldn't find my voice and I just let out some sort of moan to let him know I was more than liking it. While he did that, his other hand crawled to my aching breasts. He swiftly unhooked the frontal clasp of my bra allowing my breasts broke free of their confinements. The cool air hit

103

my nipples making them hard and aching to be licked.

My back arched as he pressed his lips onto one of my nipples. He licked and tugged at my nipple like a hungry animal. I felt more relaxed now from his touch. Finding the strength in my arms I wove my fingers into his short blond hair urging him to suck my breast harder. From the stimulation of his lips and hand it didn't take long for me to come. I grinded my pussy hard against his hand letting the pleasure wash over me.

I stood there limp for a while as I tried to catch my breath. He didn't even penetrate me and I was already having an orgasm. I felt him let go and stand in front of me. My eyes immediately went to look at the front of his pants. I started to get aroused again seeing the faint outline of his cock. I just had to touch it so I dropped onto my knees and undid the button. I pulled down the zipper and watched as his pants dropped effortlessly down to his ankles.

I could see the head of his cock peaking through the hole of his plaid boxers. Reaching out, I yanked it out of the hold and started to stroke it furiously. He was semi-hard already but I needed him fully hard. Looking up, I saw him looking down at me like I was some sort of amateur in the art of hand jobs.

"Put it in your mouth," he said.

Gripping the base, I wrapped my lips around the tip. My taste buds went crazy as I sucked him half way. His cock was so thick and long, and that was all that could fit into my little mouth. His cock tasted so good, I just wanted to suck on it for days. Soon I felt him slowly thrust his cock into my mouth creating a steady rhythm with my bobbing head.

Within minutes, his cock was rock hard in my mouth. I could feel his veins in his cock pumping blood. Moving my free hand to his balls, squeezed them and heard him grunt louder. I could feel he was close to coming.

"Stop, baby, stop," he groaned, pulling my head off his cock with his hand. I looked at his glistening cock as it stood at attention.

"Get on your feet," he instructed me and, with a bit of a struggle, I stood up.

I watched as his fingers travelled to the top of his buttoned dress shirt. His long fingers undid the buttons from the top to the bottom. With each button getting undone, I could see his bare skin. Once he was done with the unbuttoning, I placed my hands over his chest, focusing on his pierced nipples. I gently rubbed them with my fingers and tugged them gently. Moving my hands to his shoulders, I pushed the shirt out of the way. Then I raked my fingertips down his back and up again right to his hair where I pulled his head in for a steamy kiss.

The kiss was filled with deep passion. Our mouths not getting enough of each other. My tongue relished the way his moved against mine. As we kissed heavily, I felt his hand push up my skirt and move my panties to the side. Pinning me against the door again, he grabbed his cock and started to rub the tip up and down my aching pussy.

I just wanted him to stick in me already. He finally found my opening and slowly inserted himself inside me. My eyes widened with pleasure as his cock lunged forward, filling my pussy up completely. He started out thrusting slowly, allowing his cock to get used to my tight pussy. My fingers dug onto his shoulders as I enjoyed the sweet pleasure.

Gradually he started to thrust faster, banging my body over and over against the wooden door. His cock created a sweet friction against my pussy walls as he thrusted. It felt so good to have him fucking me. I moaned and grunted in pleasure as I felt my orgasm approaching. I could feel he was close too. I heard his breath coming in short, quick gasps, against my right ear. Soon the sound of our skin slapping got louder as he went faster as his cock worked in and out of me like a jackhammer.

Cries of pleasure escaped my lips while my body grew closer to a sweet release. He kept his pace and I felt my head spinning. I was going to come and I felt it was going to be intense. He gave one last sharp thrust and I felt his sperm squirt into me. It was like he couldn't stop coming as my pussy contracted and squeezed all the come out of his balls. We stayed still for a long moment letting our orgasms wash over us.

I collapsed to the ground, when he removed himself from me. I swore I still felt like I was still coming. I looked at him as he pulled up his pants and put on his shirt casually. He was back to being Mr Emotionless, acting like nothing happened. On shaky legs, I slowly stood up. I quickly put on my bra and shirt. When I was done adjusting my clothes, I looked up hoping to see him still standing there so I could give him one last hug and kiss but I noticed that he disappeared without saying good-bye, just like the other times.

I sighed, I wishing he would have swept me off my feet and take me to his bedroom so I could snuggle up against his body. Then I quickly realised that he isn't that type of man. He doesn't cuddle. He just fucks.

Waiting For Pleasure
by Lynn Rushton

He leads me down the stairs and turns me to face the wall. I try to lean back into him, but a light slap warns me that I must stand upright. He slowly slides off my blouse and bra, and I shiver as I feel the cool air against my erect nipples. The feel of the leather cuffs being fastened to my wrists sends a shock through my body. My hands are brought together and stretched high above my head and I hear the click as the cuffs are fastened to a hook in the ceiling. His hands slide gently down my arms to my shoulders and glide ever so lightly across each breast. I moan and try to arch into his hands, but the wall is in the way. His touch lingers long after his hands have moved on.

His hands continue down to my waist and I feel the silky fabric of my skirt and panties sliding down my legs. At his silent urging I lift each foot and my clothing is gone. The leather cuffs are cool against each ankle. With his foot he spreads my legs, wide and yet wider, and again I hear the click of the cuffs being snapped to hooks. I am immobile, stretched so far that I can feel the slight strain on the muscles in my legs and arms. His hands slide slowly up my legs, across my ass, still sore from my last chastisement, and linger briefly at my slit. I know he is pleased at my wetness, proof of his power over me.

He kisses my shoulder and steps back. The blindfold across my eyes pushes my concentration to my other senses. I am aware of the floor cool against the soles of my feet, the air caressing my naked body, and the leather cuffs slowly warming against my wrists and ankles. A faint chill comes off the wall inches before my face. But most of all I am aware of him standing just out of reach behind me. I am so attuned to his presence that I can hear each slight, calm breath he takes. I imagine I can feel the warmth reaching from his body. I long for his touch and try to push my ass back toward him, begging silently for a caress. He waits for my whimper of frustration before moving forward.

I abandon myself to the sensations his hands provoke. Nothing exists but the feel of his hands pinching and tugging at a nipple, sliding across my ass, a finger dipping briefly into my cunt, and gliding like a feather across my clit. I am caught between delight at his caresses and frustration that they are so gentle. When he steps back again, I protest and tug against my bonds. Another slap warns me to be still, and then I feel the gag at my lips. I open my mouth obediently as he slips it in and fastens it tightly across the back of my head. I know my protest has annoyed him. He will hear my moans and whimpers muffled through the gag, but I will no longer be able to speak to him of my need.

The clink of a chain warns me a split second before the searing fire of the clamp hits my nipple. I bite down hard on the gag, and the taste of the rubber fills my mouth. He drops the weight, and I feel its tug as he fastens the second clamp. Pain and pleasure are mingled as I feel the swaying and tug of the weight pulling against my nipples. His fingers brush against my clit in a brief reward. I know that my pleasure in the pain from

108

his hands has pleased him. The cool of the plug sliding ever so slowly into my ass is my second reward, and I moan and try to push against it. When the vibrations begin, I discover pure frustration. My bonds are too tight and I cannot move freely into the sensation.

And then I hear his footsteps receding and the door closing. He has brought me to the crest and abandoned me there, unable to touch myself, unable even to move. I am in desperation, realising that this is my punishment for my latest infraction, and with no idea how far he will take it. I strain to hear his steps, hoping that he will soon return. Each time I hear him approach the stairs, I relax thinking he is returning, only to tense again as he moves away. When I hear the faint sound of the television, I lose hope. He will not be back soon, and I am caught, balanced on the brink of orgasm, unable to approach or depart from the edge.

When he finally returns, I am sobbing silently with remorse and need. He leaves the cuffs and blindfold on as he unhooks me from the wall and removes my gag. I lean against him sobbing and pleading, kissing his neck and chest, while he gently strokes my back. He tilts my face up and tenderly kisses away my tears. I am relieved as he hushes me, leads me to a seat and pushes me down on my knees before him. I am sure that his placing my hands at his zipper signals the end of my punishment.

I lean forward, loving the feel of his cock in my hands and mouth, eager to please him, knowing that my release will come after his. He slows me down, forcing me to take my time, to make it last. With the increased concentration on his cock in my mouth, comes a new awareness of the weight at my nipples and the pulsation in my ass. I delight in the sensations flowing between these three points. But my cunt is empty and I long for something to fill it. The emptiness centres a part of my attention on my clit, and I savour its ache. I fantasise about reaching a hand down, but know that I must not. The realisation that this is his intent increases my pleasure as I kiss, and lick, and stroke him. I am so aroused that when his release finally spills into my mouth I almost come too. I moan again as I feel myself just miss orgasm, but I know that he will soon satisfy me. He has brought me to a pinnacle I had never even glimpsed before, and I am eagerly awaiting my descent from this height.

I wait quietly at his feet as he recovers, my head resting on his thigh, content that by accepting his punishment I have earned his forgiveness, and that soon I will receive my reward. When he speaks, I am startled, but I listen intently as he gives me a new rule to follow. I imagine his face as he watches my dismay. I must not ever come unless he first gives permission. I may touch myself whenever and in any way I wish unless he expressly forbids it, but I may not bring myself to orgasm without his consent. And so, I may give myself any pleasure but this most important one that he reserves for himself. I accept the rule, knowing that I have no real choice, and trusting that my quiet acceptance will increase my reward. The jolt as he drops my clothes in my lap, orders me to remove my toys and get dressed, and leaves me unsatisfied, almost undoes me. I sit alone for a long time before I begin to dress.

Adultery
by Teresa Noelle Roberts

"Tell me you're mine," I demand as I redden your golden-brown ass. "Tell me you're mine." The fingers of my other hand caress you, enter you. Spanking, stroking, I take you to the edge and hold you there until, obedient to need, you moan, "I'm yours." Only then when you have admitted you belong to me do I kiss you. Only then do I permit you to clench around me and cry out. Flushed, panting, wet, your body is not lying. In this moment you belong to me utterly.

And I dream that this time you will not leave and go home to your husband.

Sticky Notes
by Chris Bridges

Thwack! A little folded football of paper bounced off the monitor, startling the crap out of me and landing on my mouse pad. Inside, in purple ink, it said, *I wub you!*

I followed the logical trajectory across the room to see Maria sitting on the couch watching television. There was an unearthly beauty about her face and throat, reflected in the dancing blue light. She gave absolutely no impression that she was aware of me, but there was an incriminating purple marker in sight by her hand. Uh-oh. She's bored. This meant trouble.

Our tastes in casual hobbihood are very different. I prefer unwinding and relaxing by getting on the computer and cruising the net, finding cool new sites, downloading mp3s, playing games, making web pages, stuff like that, stuff that's generally a one-person activity. She likes movies, which should have meant that we were completely compatible except she liked watching movies with someone, which meant me. It's a tricky thing to explain to the love of your life that you'd rather stare at a computer than spend time with your honey, and I've yet to discover the best way to go about it. Usually, we manage.

I took the note, wrote *I wub you more!* on the back, refolded it, and casually pitched it back in her direction.

Then I turned quickly back to the computer before the note landed. There was no audible sign that the message was received. Back to work.

The next note landed squarely on the keyboard, causing a brief flurry of fhgfg's. This one read "I wub you more than all the sequins on Tina Turner." A glance – she was furiously intent on her show. My return over-the-shoulder volley read "I wub you more than all the grapes in Grapeland." I went ahead and saved the page I had been working on, since clearly this would escalate and the chances of getting any more work done were slim.

The next one hit me in the head and rolled under the desk, which made retrieving it nonchalantly an exercise in stealth. It read "I wub you more than all the fins in Finland, which is way more than the grape thing because there was a drought in Grapeland this year and they all died and it was very heartless of you to bring it up." This time when I looked over she was still facing towards the screen, but I could see muscles twitching in her neck where her giggles were being squashed.

Obviously this was going to take more direct action.

I got up and walked over to stand in front of her; she moved her head to the side with magnificent disdain to keep the TV in view. I kneeled in front of her and immediately noticed two things: one, the pile of assorted notepads stashed between her thigh and the arm of the couch, and two, she was only wearing her nightshirt. A soft, grey, stretchy nightshirt.

A course of action presented itself.

Lifting the hem of the shirt I carefully rolled it upwards, scooting it past her hips (which she coincidentally lifted just then) and over her breasts. She continued to watch the movie, to all outward appearances completely unaware that she was now barefoot up to the neck. I nuzzled that neck a bit but got no obvious reaction, so I moved downwards and began to feast on her magnificent breasts. This might not have been the attention she was looking for, but then her notes hadn't been terribly specific.

Another note came into view: *Excuse me, what are you doing?* I hadn't seen her move, which meant that either I had been more preoccupied than I thought or she had a pile of notes ready for probable eventualities. Fair enough. I kept working my way around the south slope of her left breast while reaching blindly beside her, pulling back to see a handful of sticky notes and a pen. I wrote *Nothing to see here, go about your business* and stuck it on her right nipple upside down so she could read it. It stayed solidly in place at first, but as my tongue finally reached the centre of her left tit I had an excellent view of the note pulling s-l-o-w-l-y away from her skin to accommodate the growing nipple underneath.

Clearly such a breakdown in communications would not do. I reached over and used my fingers to hold it down, pinning her nipple underneath. A small circular motion seemed indicated to help keep it in place.

She began to move against my hand. A quick glance upwards showed that she was still watching the screen, seemingly unaware of me, but the sweet humidity coming from below argued otherwise. I let go of the note and everything stopped as I watched it tugging at her skin, millimetre by millimetre, before it finally pulled free to perch atop a very rigid nipple. When I looked up she was still staring straight ahead, but her eyes were very bright.

I tongued my way around her tummy and bellybutton, occasionally dipping into the thatch of soft curls below.

114

A pressure on my hand caught my attention; there was a note stuck there: *Lick slowly.* I let my grin sink between her spreading thighs. The sight and the smell of her hit me hard, like it always does, and I could feel the familiar boil rolling through my bloodstream. Drops of moisture were appearing along the soft fleshy ridges between her legs, so I used my tongue to gather them together and spread them more evenly. I'm a helpful kind of guy. Slowly, as per instructions, I licked up and down and around and through and back and forth and all of it all over again. Her legs eased away from either side of my head, tugging her lips apart with a moist sound, and I dove for the sharper tastes to be found deep inside.

I almost laughed out loud when the next note appeared. It said, in shaky handwriting, *Ahh!* She had yet to make a sound, so that became my goal.

Her juices dripped down my chin. I licked up into her, straining my tongue and my jaw to hit the right spot, and was rewarded with a frantic wiggle and what sounded suspiciously like a person biting her own arm to stay quiet. The *Ahhh!* note was joined with a new one: *AHHH GOD!* I took the new note and, placing it squarely over the bulging bud of her clit, stabbed it in place with my tongue. Her heels pounded on my back and her hips thrust forward, so I did it again.

And again.

And again, finally pinning the note and swirling it around as fast as I could. Notes began raining down over her thighs as she lost control and I chuckled into her pussy when I read some of the situations she had been prepared for. *Not so fast*, *Use your teeth*, *Harder, Eduardo, harder* (my name is Tony), *Oh God, my husband!* (we're not married), *Eat me, you Scandinavian stud!* (I'm American), *I'm coming!* and more.

115

I took the last one and stuck it on my forehead so she could see it while I took the soggy note over her clit, and her clit, between my lips and munched happily away. But even as I felt her rocking into her pre-orgasm build-up, I decided she needed something extra.

I grabbed the fat purple marker. It was a Sharpee with smooth rounded edges on the cap, which was good because I didn't want to hurt her when I shoved it up into her slit and held it firm against the upper inside of her cunt. Her hands clutched the sides of the couch and she bore down hard, forcing the marker against the right spot. I attacked her clit with hungry glee and was rewarded with silent screams from above and a neck-breaking orgasm exploding around me.

I licked her through it, lapping more gently as the waves subsided, until I was nuzzling the inside of her thighs and catching my breath. A new pre-written note appeared, displaying an admirable prophetic ability.

Thank you. Get that thing out of me.

I let the pen drop into my hand and wiped it on my shirt. Then I rose up to sit next to her. Maria was drenched in sweat, her thick curly hair plastered to her face, and she still had her nightgown bunched up against her neck. Her breasts were full and jiggling from her panting. Her legs were still spread wide. Her eyes, fixed on the direction of the TV, were lidded and sensual. She was the sexiest thing I had ever seen, and there was only one thing left to do.

I reached over, plucked the notepad from her side and started writing notes.

For the first time all night, Maria turned to look at me and smiled, waiting.

Taxi!
by Simon Keen

They walked from the dinning tables into the ballroom together, hand in hand. He wore an evening suit with a deep red lining. She wore a classic black evening dress, split up the side, strapless and shaped to her body. Although both in their late forties they oozed sex appeal. The confidence they showed was a confidence in their own characters and in the closeness they still had after 25 years of marriage. They held hands like young lovers, as if they were inseparable.

The ballroom was already full of people, some dancing and some sitting at the scattered tables. As CEO of the company his main task was to mingle. She knew that and assumed the same duty. He leant over to her as they walked and whispered "Here we go". He said it gently, allowing his breath to caress the inside of her ear, she felt the warmth run into her chest. As he finished he darted the very tip of his tongue into her ear, sending a small electric pulse through her. Neither of them broke step as they parted with this small exchange of sensation. They headed for opposite sides of the room, engaging the first groups they met.

As they moved around the room they exchanged glances. He looked across at the way her dress clung to her hips, imagining later when he would hold them as they moved rhythmically in each others arms. She looked at his face, the warmth of it, the way he smiled so much. She had always loved his face and often lay at night watching it as he slept.

They met up at the back of the room; they had been apart for three hours. They both knew the decorum required at these events but delighted in secret excesses. They stood opposite each other and reached for the others hand. To everyone else it was a gentle meeting between a middle-aged couple. But as he placed his hand in hers he leaned towards her and whispered.

"I want to slide your dress up over your arse and fuck you slowly from behind."

A mischievous smile darted across her face as she replied, "It's lucky I don't have knickers on then."

Neither of them would ordinarily swear but that made their sex talk even more of a turn on. They adored sex together and always had. They were very happily married and had loved each other deeply for many years. Never had either thought the adoration of the others body was instead of love. They knew that the deep lust they felt for each other was because of their love.

A guest approached, obviously intent on engaging the husband in conversation. She smiled at the guest and, as she turned, she trailed her hand gently over the front of her husband's trousers. Gently enough so the movement didn't draw attention but firmly enough so his cock could feel her through his trousers.

The evening drew to a close and the guests left. The couple were the last to leave, climbing into a taxi that would take them to their hotel for the night. Both of them were tired from the evening's duties but as they sat together the pheromones mingled. It was the early hours of the morning, the streets were almost empty and the back of a black cab seemed romantic. The cabby was quiet and inside the cab was dark. They sat close together against the side of the cab directly behind the driver. She half turned so that she could kiss her husband full on the lips. She did so gently at first but with growing pressure and fervour.

Her hand moved to his lap, she caressed his cock through his trousers.

As the kisses grew so did the caresses, from a gentle stroke until she was firmly grasping his cock and sliding her hand down around his balls. He ran his hand up her thigh but, although the dress was split up the side, it was far too tight to venture under, so his hand quickly made its way to her breast. He squeezed her breast through the fabric of the dress.

"We have never fucked in a taxi," she said quietly but with a spark of excitement in her voice.

The journey to the hotel was only 15 minutes long and they were almost there. He leant forward and spoke to the driver.

"We aren't in the mood for going to the hotel yet. Would you mind driving around for a while?"

"No problems, mate, you're paying," the taxi driver replied. He must have known what was about to happen because he shut the small glass window that was perpetually open between the driver and the passengers.

As her husband sat back into the rear seat, she lifted herself up and slid her dress up so that he arse was bare and in contact with the seat. As she sat back down she spread her legs enough to allow his hand to find her already hot and wet pussy. He had always loved the first touch of her pussy and tonight it seemed hotter than normal and already dripping wet. His finger slid between her lips and started long, slow, firm strokes from the rose of her arse to the tip of her clit. She tugged at his flies, cursing the fact that they always resisted being undone by anyone but the wearer. Eventually she had his trousers undone. His rubbing on her pussy had brought her close to orgasm and she wasted no time. She thrust her hand into his trousers and pulled out his cock so that it was in full view. It was hard and eager. She pushed back his trousers making sure the zip would not catch him and grabbed his cock again in her fist. There was not going to be much foreplay this time. She gave his cock three strong strokes but could not wait any longer. Standing as best as she could in the cab, 'Thank god for London cabs' she thought, she turned her back towards him, holding her dress up so that her arse and the slick wet edge of her pussy could just be seen in the subdued light. She lowered herself down onto his cock. He slid forwards on the seat to enter her better and deeper. The heat of her pussy surged around his cock and he tried hard to suppress a strong moan as he entered her. She closed her legs slightly and sat between his. With her hands on his thighs she started to ride him, not slowly and gently but as if she was riding a wild horse. She thrust up and down hard until she came suddenly. She stopped moving, suspended on her arms she held her breath, the scream held inside her chest instead of thrown out as she wanted.

After a few seconds, she relaxed and lowered herself down onto his cock. As she looked up she caught sight of the cabby's eyes darting between the road and his rear view mirror. She smiled a warm smile at him. She wasn't an exhibitionist but didn't mind, he had after all contributed to her pleasure. When he saw the smile he looked quickly ahead, embarrassed.

As she recovered from her pleasure she realised her

husband's cock was still inside her. He hadn't come and his hard on was starting to subside with the shift from frantic fucking to sitting. She lifted herself off him, feeling her wet pussy give his cock up. She turned and squatted, her dress gathered on her lap. She grasped his cock in her right hand while steadying herself against the seat with her left. His cock was wet with her juice. She looked up at him with a wicked smile and then slid his cock into her mouth. He straightened in the seat as his muscles stiffened. She started to move rhythmically up and down. Grasping his cock she kept her hand in time with her mouth. She held him hard so that he had the pressure to make him come quickly and powerfully, whilst letting him feel the warmth and softness of her mouth. His cock quickly regained it stiffness as she slid more rapidly up and down. She loved him coming in her mouth and became carried away with the movement. When he came she sucked the cum into her throat and swallowed it eagerly, dragging as much out as possible. He flinched as she continued to work his cock. His hands were screwed into fists and his thigh muscles tensed solid. She lifted her head and smiled at him.

She tucked his cock gently into his trousers, did up his flies and stood up as best she could. Letting her dress drop as she turned to the cabby, she opened the glass partition and said, "The Savoy, please."

Kissing Booth
by Lynn Burton

I watched Maddie hammer nails into boards, one after another, as if it was the most natural thing for her to do. And she did make it look natural. Her slender hand wrapped around the handle of the hammer, bang, bang, banging nails until they were safely embedded deep in the wood.

When the booth was complete, she went to work on the sign for the front of it. With careful strokes, she painted the words "Kissing Booth" in bold red letters. She sat back admiring her work and then a smile softened her features as she added "25 cents" underneath.

From my seat on her couch, I shook my head. "This is probably the dumbest idea you've ever had, you know that?"

She frowned at me. Pretending that my comment bothered her, she said, "Thanks for your support."

I couldn't help but smile then, too, at the small streak of red paint on her cheek and the way some strands of black hair were plastered to her forehead. "You're welcome."

Maddie went right back to work on her paint job and I continued to watch. She didn't care what I thought. She was completely happy with the idea that our adult male friends would find paying for a kiss to be amusing.

As if she could read my mind, she said, "The guys are going to love this. It's not just your average kissing booth."

"No?"

Obviously proud of herself, Maddie smiled and then went on to explain. "No. Whoever is the best kisser gets to kiss me somewhere else." Her eyes went all dark and mischievous.

Interesting to say the least. And that was Maddie-interesting, in a most pleasant way.

Pleasant in the way she beamed at me over her latest idea of turning something innocent into something ... not so innocent. And pleasant in the way her white tank top clung to her sticky skin after hours of work. Maddie hardly ever wore a bra. Not that she needed to, with breasts as perfect as hers. I even had the size and shape fixed in my mind.

I was licking my lips and daydreaming about what they'd taste and feel like in my mouth when I heard Maddie say, "Why don't you come over here and see if you think everything looks OK?"

Our eyes locked and stayed that way while I lifted myself off the couch and walked towards her.

"Were you staring at my breasts, Cass?" she asked as casual as could be.

I didn't answer. I couldn't. My voice was lost somewhere between a vision of her breasts and the slow heat rising inside me. I just stood there trying not to look at them again, but damn, it was hard.

"Cassandra."

I've always loved the sound of my name coming from Maddie's lips. If I waited long enough to answer, maybe she'd say it again.

But she did more than say my name. Without so much

as another word, Maddie took off her sweat soaked tank top to expose the breasts that I'd fantasised about since the first time we met.

"Maybe we can get this kissing booth started off right," Maddie cooed.

And that was all the invitation I needed. My hands cupped the perfect mounds. Maddie's soft sighs only excited me more and I ran my palms in a circular motion over each breast. My reward was a hard, pink nipple. So pretty.

Maddie grabbed the back of my hair and pulled me to one breast.

My tongue flicked out hungrily, taking one proud nipple into my mouth and then the other. They tasted better than I could've ever imagined and I wanted to kiss them forever.

While I was bathing her breasts with my tongue, Maddie unzipped her cut off jean shorts and slid them down her long, slender legs. I took my mouth away only for a moment to admire the heaven between them.

Maddie grabbed my shoulders and pushed me down on my knees. So hungry and eager to please, I ran my hands up her thighs and slid my thumbs over her outer lips. The smell of her arousal hung in the air and I couldn't wait another minute to taste her there too.

I tested the wetness with my fingers, sliding easily inside her. She moaned and pulled on my hair hard enough to jerk my head back so I was looking directly up at her.

My own pussy throbbed and ached at seeing the pleasure on her face.

When she eased her grip on my hair, I put my face back where it belonged. Right on her glistening pussy.

With two slick fingers working inside her, I rolled my

tongue around her clit, bit it and sucked it. I slid my fingers out and reached up so Maddie could taste herself. Watching her wrap her gorgeous lips around my fingers wet with her own juices was too much. I took my hand away so I could have both of them free to grab her ass and pull her closer, latching onto her hot treasure again with my mouth.

It wouldn't take long now. I could feel the pressure building. She was so close and I wanted her to come. Wanted her juices to spill out into my mouth so I could drink and taste, cherish the sweetness.

"Oh, God," she was saying as the waves crashed over her body, hitting her, rolling over and over again. And then there was the sound of something hitting glass.

In our own fantasy world, Maddie and I hadn't heard anyone else enter the room until we turned to see our friends smiling and emptying their pockets of change for our kissing booth.

The Gym
by Sabrina Ingram

I've been watching him for a while.

He is the motivation that keeps me going back to the gym.

Exercising isn't something I enjoy but when I can watch him in the mirror as I run on the treadmill it's not only sweat that dampens my body. The sight of his sleek muscles straining as he adds more weight to the barbells and lays back on the bench to do more presses gives me ideas on other ways we could work out together on that very same bench.

I fantasise that we're the only people in the gym and I use his safety straps to restrain his hands on the barbell above him. Then I stand next to the bench and strip off my sweaty workout clothes, slowly revealing myself to him. The tent in his shorts caused by his straining erection encourages me to take total control of his body.

Walking to the end of the bench I lean over his body, just close enough to brush the hard tips of my breasts against his bare stomach. I let my head fall so that my long hair brushes against his firm chest, tickling him as I lightly swing my head back and forth. Then I lower my body closer so that my tits now hug his cock through his shorts and he feels my hot breath on his chest. I open my mouth and my tongue darts out to tease his nipple to erectness. When it's sticking up like a miniature cock I take the hard nub into my wet mouth and nibble teasingly with my teeth. Then I lave it better with firm strokes of my tongue. I shift slightly for better access to the other nipple and the shift of pressure on his cock causes him to lift his hips against me and groan softly. He doesn't want to speak any more than I want to hear him, his groans and sighs are message enough.

When both nipples are standing proud, wet and shiny from my ministrations, I slide my body back so I am on my knees between his. Leaning back, I quickly divest him of his shorts so that his throbbing cock is bare and only inches from my hungry lips.

Liking the power I feel with him laid out before me I tease a little more. I lean forward and nip at his inner thigh with my sharp teeth, knowing that as I do this all he really feels is the inching of my fingers through the nest of curls at the base of his cock. To get his focus where I want it, I push his thighs further apart and place a long wet lick with firm pressure on that soft skin between his puckered asshole and his heavy balls. He tries to lift his hips and increase the pressure, but I deny him that.

After sucking his balls into my hot mouth for a brief taste I decide I'm done teasing.

I can feel my own juices starting to run from my swollen pussylips down my thighs as I pull his cock away from his belly and surround it with my lips. After a minute of adjustment I start a slow rhythm of bobbing with my mouth giving firm suction. He tastes delicious, salty and sweet.

The sounds coming from his throat as I speed up slightly are causing my quim to quiver in anticipation. One of my hands leaves his thigh to reach between mine to play with myself. As I slip a finger deep inside I realise it isn't enough so I add another. This isn't what I want. I want to be filled and that's for him to do.

Abandoning all my ministrations I stand up and quickly straddle him on the bench. I don't move until he opens his eyes and is watching me. With eyes held I reach between my spread legs and guide him into my wet hole. I lower myself and we both let out a groan of satisfaction as his hard rigid cock fills me.

I start to roll my hips gently and notice that his grip on the barbell above him has become white knuckled. I lean forward and place my hands next to his on the barbell and start to pump my hips faster. With feet flat on the floor, I have total control and ease with shifting tempo and pressure on him.

The air is still around us, only disturbed by our panting breath and the occasional grunt and groan from him. I squeeze him tight inside and know that he can't hold back much longer. I pump a little faster.

The end is near for us both. I tilt my hips to that angle I know will get him deeper and give my throbbing clit the pressure I need to get off. A quick thrust and our hips grind together and I feel myself slip into oblivion. My inner walls clench around his throbbing cock as he shoots into me hotly, filling me the way I've fantasised about.

With no strength left in my body I release my grip on the barbell, undo the ties that bind his wrists and cuddle up on the chest I've admired for so long as his arms surround me.

He is the inspiration that keeps me going to the gym.

Nice Kitty Kat
by Michelle Houston

It never failed. I agree to something without knowing the whole story and find myself in the oddest of situations. Last time a friend of mine needed my help, I wound up driving him and his friends back from a gay bachelor party. Seems he felt it was best for a woman to drive around a bunch of shit-faced gay men.

Now this. Laughing softly to myself, I had to admit that this was definitely the strangest of outcomes, agreeing to be a friend's 'date' to a costume party. Memo to self: next time, get costume veto approval, and find out exactly where the party was being held.

When Carmen showed up at my house two hours ago and held out a box, sense she was dressed in a tux, I figured I would be the bride. How wrong I was.

Inside the deceptively simple box was a set of body paints, a T back thong, a collar, and a set of cat ears. Arching my brow at her, I had to ask just what she had planned. Now, I wish I hadn't.

Squirming slightly, I tried to ease the pressure of Carmen's friend's hands against my ass, but the woman was determined that I stay put. A quick slap to my bare ass quickly drove that point home.

"Be a good pussy now," Anne, the bitch goddess from hell, cooed. Carmen sure could pick them. First, she introduces me to a cross-dresser who simply had to borrow my lipstick, then to a woman so far in the closet she was attached to a hanger, and now a full time Domme.

"Yes, Mistress," I whispered, laying my head against her thigh. Here I was, a grown woman, who ran a successful business, lying almost naked over a strange woman's lap. I felt her hands gently stroked down my spine, which I had to admit felt nice, once I got used to the feel of her leather pants against my stomach.

"Katrina, are you enjoying the party?"

I couldn't help but glare at Carmen. She sat comfortably next to a petite blonde dressed in a virginal white nightgown, which left next to nothing to the imagination. Yet here I was, butt-ass naked.

"Yeah, loads. This is just how I imagined my Saturday night. Seriously though, when's this thing end?"

"In a couple of hours." I would have bitched and protested, but the "bride" chose that moment to get jealous and drag Carmen out on the dance floor. I could have cheerfully yanked her dyed hair out – after all, it was her royal highness' fault I was bullied into being Carmen's date.

"You're not enjoying yourself, my little Kitty Kat?" Those magical hands danced back up my spine as Anne spoke.

"To be honest, not really. Why is it again that I can't get up?"

Anne laughed softly. I found my thong growing a bit damp at the husky sound of her voice. I didn't want to be attracted to her, she was way out of my sexual league, but there was something about her that I couldn't resist.

"Because, darling, I own you. Carmen and I traded – Julie for you." Her voice deepened with the last words.

Trembling slightly, I tried to deny the effect her voice was having on me. Focusing on how I must look to everyone in the room helped some.

"Let's see if I can help you enjoy yourself a bit more." Her words should have warned me, but I never expected her to pull my thong aside and shove two fingers up my creaming cunt.

"Mmmmm," I heard myself moaning, before I could stop. I wanted to relax into her touch, but a laugh across the room reminded me that we were most definitely not alone.

"Stop that," I demanded, my body screaming for more. "Someone could see you."

Anne's fingers slipped free and I breathed a sigh of relief, too quickly. Her hand landed with a solid smack against my ass.

"Ouch!" I exclaimed softly.

"Let me make something very clear my little pussy. No one cares what I do to you, so long as I don't hurt you. That's why we have these parties. Now, if you don't like something I do, you can object. Just don't pretend that you aren't wet for my touch."

After having her say, she landed another smack against my already tender ass. I squirmed on her lap at the harsh sting. For some weird reason, the sting in my ass only made my cunt wetter. I could feel my mons sliding along wet leather as my juices dripped onto her pants.

Before the sting of the swat softened, her fingers slid back into my pussy. Arching slightly, I silently begged for more. I wasn't sure why I was even willing to let her continue, but even knowing people could be, would be watching, I wanted more.

If I were honest with myself, which at the moment, I

131

couldn't do, I would have admitted to the fact that people was watching only added to the appeal.

As her fingers slightly withdrew, then firmly thrust in again, I tried to lie still. I didn't want to do anything to attract attention to myself. My resolve didn't last long though. After her fourth thrust, I couldn't have cared less. The bitch knew just where to touch, just what pressure to apply, to have me sobbing for more.

I lay there, sprawled across her lap, and let her finger me into a screaming orgasm. It was only as applause filled the room that my concern about spectators returned. I knew I had to be blushing beet red – my face was certainly hot enough. While fighting to calm my racing pulse, I turned my face into Anne's inner thigh and tried to wait out the storm.

It didn't happen.

Shouts of, "Encore! Encore!" forced me to admit to the fact – no one was just going to return to their business.

Anne's hands settled on my shoulders and gently pushed. I fell softly onto the floor. Rolling over, I got to my knees and was preparing to stand when a high-heeled leather boot pressed against my shoulder.

"Not so fast, Kitty Kat. It's my turn now." The foot slid down my shoulder, all the way to my elbow, then returned to the floor.

Shocked, I turned to face her and found myself eye level with her crotch. When her legs were pressed together, her leather pants looked solid, but as she parted her legs a tiny slit of material was missing; just enough to bare her pussy.

"Now, my little pussy."

I couldn't help but find her smooth shaven flesh alluring. The creamy peach of her skin glistened in the muted light of the club.

"Don't make me spank you, Kat. I said, now."

'Bitch' I though, but wasn't daring enough to say it. 'Beautiful, sexy, seductive bitch.' Heaven help me, I wanted her. I was quivering inside, imagining how sweet her pussy would taste. I wanted to lick her cunt from top to bottom; I wanted to tongue her puckered asshole. Whatever she needed, I wanted to give her.

I crawled forward and laid my head on her thigh, inhaling deeply of her fragrance. A heady musk filled my senses. Tentatively, I lapped at her pussy lips, before stabbing deeply into her pussy. Anne's hands fisted in my hair as I pulled back and thrust again.

"More, you little tease," she demanded. "Don't make me whip you."

While the idea was slowly gaining in appeal, the reality of her juices coating my tongue won out and I doubled my efforts to fuck Anne to a creaming orgasm.

I could hear the faint hum of conversations all around as I tongued the leather-clad Domme, but I tuned them out. All that mattered to me in those moments was the feel of her velvety flesh squeezing my tongue.

If I had known Anne better, the subtle signs would have alerted me – but as it was, I had no warning before she climaxed, flooding my mouth with her musky essence.

My cunt twitched as I swallowed her juices.

Oddly breathless, I laid my head against her thigh again and waited, wondering whether she wanted more.

Her fingers untangled from my hair, and she gently smoothed the tangled tresses. "That's a good little kitty," she purred.

"No come up here and curl up in my lap."

Legs trembling, I stood and watched as she pressed

133

her legs together again. The illusion of decency returned, but I knew how quickly that could change. Kneeling on the couch next to her, I curled against her side, my back to her. Her smooth hands slowly stroked up and down my spine, petting me.

"Now, look over there. See you aren't the only one who's being watched tonight. At some time or another, everyone is in the spotlight."

Across the room, Carmen ripped Julie's nightgown from her petite form. Strangers shackled her to a large cross, her back to the crowd. As Carmen removed her pants, I could see a familiar harness buckled to her slender form. Accepting a whip from one audience member, she allowed another to attach a cock to her harness. Moments later, Julie's moans and gasps reached my ears as Carmen alternately whipped and fucked her lover.

Curling tighter to Anne's side, I began to plot how I was going to get Carmen to bring me as her date again

Room Service
by Rosewater Elf

I know I am gonna get fired for this – but I don't care! He is worth it. I knock tentatively on his door. I have followed his career for ages and I am not gonna miss my one and only chance at getting what I want from him.

"Who is it?" the warm, slightly accented voice calls.

"Room Service," I reply, opening another button on my blouse.

I am smoothing my skirt over my thighs as the door opens.

"Hello …" he says with a mixture of surprise and delight, "can I help you?"

Pausing before I answer, I allow my gaze to wander idly down his impressive height.

"I certainly hope so …"

A puzzled look crosses his handsome features. Realising that I need to make myself a little clearer, I walk up closer to him.

"I have seen you looking at me," I say boldly. "Every time you come to my reception desk, you undress me with your eyes."

He is about do deny it so I cut him off quickly, "I feel your eyes on my ass every time I walk past you …" Leaving the sentence hanging, I look up at him, waiting for a response.

Disbelief quickly followed by amusement flickers across his features. His bemused smile emboldens me and I continue.

"You look at me as if you want to take me right there, in front of everyone, right over the desk …" His mouth drops slightly open at this. He can't believe what he is hearing. One more deep breath and I take the plunge.

"… and I just wondered if I you want to do anything about it." Trailing my finger slowly down the centre of his chest for emphasis, I wait, holding my breath.

I see him weighing it up in his mind. He drops his head to look down at my finger which has come to rest on the waistband of his jeans. Raising his head, his eyes narrow and he looks at me intently.

"What do you mean?" he asks warily. The spark in his eyes tells me he knows the answer. He just needs to make real sure he has understood me.

"Come on," I drawl, "You're a big boy. You know what I mean". I smile at him indulgently. Long seconds pass and he just stares at me, giving nothing away.

My confidence is fading fast as we stand there. Maybe he does not want to do anything about it? Maybe he just likes to look??

I take a step away from him, brain scrabbling for a way to get out of this fast. Settling for bravado, I shrug my shoulders.

"OK, my mistake," I say brightly, beginning to turn away from him.

His sudden movement forward catches me by surprise. His hand grabs mine and he drags me quickly in through the open doorway, sticking his head briefly back out through it to check the hall is clear.

He shuts the door and leans into it, taking a moment to compose himself. When he finally turns to me, the wary look is back in his eye.

"Do you do this kind of thing often?" He is still unsure.

"Only when gorgeous men with dirty eyes give me horny dreams for a week"

He laughs at this, finally beginning to relax. "And how often does that happen?" he grins.

"Including this time ... once," I sass back. This amuses him again.

"I waited for you to make a move," I explain, "but nothing happened and you are leaving the Hotel tonight. So I took things into my own hands."

His gaze has darkened slightly, he is not listening to me. "What kind of dreams ... exactly?"

All the humour has gone from his expression. He watches me intently. I turn and walk to the window. Pulling the curtains as I speak, I tell him.

"Oh, you know. Your average, run of the mill fantasy stuff. Throwing you down on the bed, ripping your clothes off and fucking you senseless". It shocks me to hear these words coming out of my mouth, but he did ask! His chuckle makes me turn around to look at him.

"And how does it start?" He dares me.

"Like this," I say and give him a gentle shove back onto the bed.

He plays along and throws himself right back onto it, grinning up at me. He props himself up on his elbows to watch me advance towards him.

"What happens next?" He is enjoying this.

"Well," I reply, kneeling into the space between his thighs to unbutton his jeans, "How expensive is that shirt?"

He knows what is coming next.

"Very," he says, his tone telling me he is saying

goodbye to it.

"Pity!" Grabbing the tails in both hands, I rip it open. We both laugh as the buttons fly over us.

"And now?"

"Now, these have to go"

I stand and grab a handful of his jeans at the back of his thighs and tug hard. His body jerks with the motion of me ripping the denim down his legs. Tugging them off the end of his bare feet, I stop to admire my progress. He must have thrown some clothes on just to answer the door as he is totally naked under his jeans.

He shrugs off what is left of his shirt and throws it behind him. Resting back on his elbows, he waits. I am in no hurry, he looks gorgeous laying there. His massive cock lays dangerously against his thigh.

"Do I get to rip your clothes off in this dream?" he asks, hopefully.

"No, you lie there while I strip for you." Starting to unbutton my blouse, I continue, laughing, "I have to go back to work afterwards".

He chuckles at this and props his head on arms now folded behind his head. His expression becomes more serious as my barely covered breasts come into view. The push up bra doing its job well, my boobs threaten to spill out of the black lace cups as I lean over to drop my folded blouse on the chair.

He does not take his eyes off them as I wriggle myself out of my skirt. Dropping that onto the chair, I speak again.

"In my fantasy, you want me to keep my stockings and suspenders on as they drive you crazy."

I smooth out invisible creases in my stocking tops to focus his eyes on them. His look tells me I am right.

"You'll like the next bit," I promise him as I slide up

138

his body to kiss him.

Kneeling over him, I place my mouth on his. His lips feel just as I imagined them, warm and firm.

I move to lie down beside him, he stops me, bringing his arms around to pin me on top of him. Holding my head firmly, he raises up to take control of my mouth. He rolls over suddenly, pinning me onto the bed. Raising his head, he sees my surprise.

"In your fantasy, did you expect me to lie here totally passive?" he asks, "because that is not going to happen"

"Well, to be honest, we never actually got this far," I admit, grinning sheepishly. "Can we sort of … play it by ear?"

"Is there any other way?" He emphasises his point by dropping his head and sucking my earlobe between his teeth.

"And you were right about the stockings," he says as he moves down the bed "except you won't be needing these." And with that, he rips my briefs off.

"Hey! I have to work soon!" I exclaim. His dirty laugh fills the room.

"I love the thought of you looking so proper behind your desk minus your underwear. I am indulging a little fantasy of my own," he says, parting my thighs.

Kneeling on the floor between my feet, he reaches forward, hooks a hand under my knees and drags my ass to the edge of the bed.

"Did you imagine that I would do this …?" He asks as he licks slowly up my crease.

"And this …" as he starts to fuck me with his finger.

I can't answer him, my body is taut, hands grabbing at the covers.

"Did you know you would be this wet? And that I would love it?"

He groans as he bends down to taste me. I put my hands down to his head, holding him there. He continues to drive me crazy with his tongue and fingers. I feel my peak building, I am gonna cum soon. Suddenly he stops, getting to his feet.

"Would you indulge another little fantasy of mine?" he asks me, walking across the room to sit on a chair.

I say yes. He can have anything he wants as long as he makes me cum soon.

"Bring yourself off while I watch you."

I am not sure about this, I have never done it in front of anyone before. The thought excites me though, especially as I see him begin to idly rub himself, his eyes fixed on my pussy.

I close my eyes, unable to look at his face as I slowly trail my hand down. I jump as I touch myself, still incredibly hot from him. I am still wet from his mouth as I slide my fingers over my clit. I hear him gasp, this spurs me on and I prop my feet on the bed to give him a better view.

I open my eyes to look over at him. His face is rigid with fascination at what I am doing. I love his eyes on me. I start to cum, unable to stop myself from crying out. I rub myself wildly as I orgasm, legs trembling, my body shuddering.

I hear him come back to the bed. I watch him as he puts on a condom. His eyes are still on me as my breathing slows. He picks me up and throws me further up onto the pillows. On top of me before I land fully, he hauls one of my legs over his arm and forces his way in to my swollen wetness. He is huge. Tears prick the corners of my eyes as he fills me.

He kisses me, beginning to grunt as he thrusts into me. He drops his head down and speaks words I cant understand – God, they sound dirty though.

It is hard to believe but I feel like I am gonna cum again. He is gentle but that is not what I want. It is my turn to demand something. I reached down and slap his ass.

"In my fantasy, you fucked me hard", I growl into his ear. "Do it!"

He pauses only to hook my other leg further over his hip and speeds up. That is more like it. I push back against his thrusting, needing him inside me as far as he can go. I start to cum, harder than before.

I can hear his grunts coming closer and closer together until they meld into one long, low groan. His body jerks into me, hands almost painful on my hips as he holds me to him. He shudders to a halt, panting.

He rolls off immediately. Reaching over he pulls me to his side. Kissing his cheek, I ask him if it is OK to take a shower. He nods, smiling at me sleepily.

I am careful not to wet my hair. Maybe I can get away with this if I go back to work now. The boss may not have come looking for me yet, I hope.

I put my clothes on in the bathroom. As I open the door, a gentle snore greets me. That suits me fine, I can leave without any awkward silences and my shift will be over before he checks out.

I give his sleeping form one long last look as I close the door to the suite. It had been so much more than my limited imagination could ever have expected.

I make my way quickly back down to the desk. Sophie opens her eyes wide as she sees me and points over her shoulder to the office. I speed up, breaking into a slight run.

"It is ok, Godzilla has only just arrived," she tells me as I reach her. "I told her you were in the bathroom.

Where did you get to anyway?"

My little story about needing to lie down as I felt nauseous seems to satisfy her and I distract her with the register.

Smiling to myself, and resolving to pop into the hotel boutique for some more underwear on my next break, I get back to work.

Enough's Enough
by Monica Lamb

I do it everywhere, all over the house, whenever I can. I come four, five, six times a day, and that's just on weekdays. I'm 46 years old and I masturbate like a teenager, and I can't possibly imagine cutting back any time soon. Because I believe that enough's enough. And I haven't had nearly enough.

Maybe it's because I got the house – not that you wanted it, really, with your new girlfriend and her kids and all. Maybe it's because this house has so many rooms in it, rooms where for years I lived and worked and existed without the faintest thought of my own pleasure.

Maybe it's because I spent so many years doing the laundry in the laundry room without even thinking for an instant about stripping off my clothes, thrusting my pussy against the washing machine, and riding the spin cycle to multiple orgasms. Maybe it's because I spent so many evenings taking clean dishes out of the dishwasher and didn't ever take the time – it never occurred to me, really – to do it naked, so I could spank myself with each spatula and wooden spoon before placing it in the drawer, laughing at how it felt.

Maybe it's because I spent long nights in that big bed next to you, wondering why we weren't making love –

and I'm well beyond wondering that any more, because frankly I don't care. It never occurred to me to kick you out and stretch out in the bed with a vibrator to satisfy me. Maybe if it had you wouldn't be gone, but I'm well beyond wondering that, too – besides, I like it alone in that big bed, and the vibrator doesn't take up as much room as you did.

Maybe I do it so much because of all the years I spent looking out at the back yard and I never even thought of sunbathing nude out there – mothers and wives don't do that sort of thing, I thought, or maybe it never even really occurred to me to try it. The summers are beautiful here, and there's nothing like the feeling of warm sun and a cool breeze across my flesh as I come for the fourth time that day. Maybe I do it because in those years of watching the kids play in the back yard sprinklers, I never imagined I would one day be able to run out there on a hot day and run through them myself, stark naked, giggling like a schoolgirl as the cold water streamed against my face and breasts and pussy.

Maybe I spend so much time masturbating because of the work I did on the big computer with its 20-inch screen, balancing our chequebook, never wondering why, exactly, you needed such a big screen on your computer. Now I know, and am I ever glad you did. Maybe it's because of the years I spent emailing friends and relatives with updates about Carrie and Mike Jr., how Mike's Junior Varsity team had won, how Carrie had gotten her first 4.0 at Dartmouth, without even once realising that I could log in to chatrooms and tell a bunch of people exactly what I was doing with one hand while I typed with the other, or get obscene emails from men I'd never met describing to me what they'd do with their mouths if I was there in front of them.

Maybe it's the fantasies I never had of you fucking me on the dining room table after a romantic candlelight dinner – I never had them, at least, until you were gone, and something weird about that made them even more delicious and more taboo. Maybe it's the fantasies I never had about doing it on the couch with the curtains open, or the videos you hid in the back of the closet that I never had the guts to watch on the wide-screen TV in the living room – until after you'd moved out and forgot a couple.

Maybe it's all those reasons, or maybe it's just that I finally realised that I *could.* After all, I loved you for so many years, and for some of them it was incredible. For most of the rest, it was just fine, and for the last few, it was harder than anything I've ever had to face.

So you're gone, now, and it would be strange that I don't miss you – if, for all those years of making it work between us, I didn't kind of miss myself.

You said it yourself, two days after our 23rd anniversary, in our millionth session with Dr. Parker. You summed it all up, I guess, when you said "Monica, you know it and I know it. Enough's enough."

And it is. Enough was most certainly enough between you and me. And enough is enough for me, now, alone in this big house with more pleasure to bring myself than I ever knew I could be brought. Enough is, definitely, enough.

And I'll let you know if I ever get there.

145

Window Of Opportunity
by Michelle Houston

"Ms Collins. There's a Nina Paterson here to see you. And Mr Andrews wanted me to remind you that the window washers are working on our side of the building today."

Looking up from the piles of papers covering her desk, Amanda Collins answered into the speakerphone. "Thank you Cindy. Send her right in. And why don't you go ahead and take lunch?"

"Thank you, Ms Collins. I'll be back in an hour." As Cindy's words came out of the speaker Amanda's door swung open and a tall redhead stepped across the threshold.

Leaning back in her seat, Amanda Collins watched her lover lock the door and cross the room. Perfectly dressed in a skirt suit and heels, she had an air of respectability. But Amanda knew that underneath the facade, Nina's lingerie was lacy trimmed silken sin – if she was even wearing any.

"Miss me, lover?"

"Definitely. But what are you doing here? I have a meeting in about forty minutes. I told you this morning, I'm busy today, and can't leave for lunch."

Nina took her time in answering. She walked around Amanda's desk and perched on the edge of the burnished walnut top, crossing her silk stocking-clad legs.

"I just thought since you're working so hard and have such a busy day that you might like a nice massage. Or maybe something a bit more relaxing."

"Nina, love, I don't think that this is the time or place."

Nina shook her head, sending a cascade of red curls floating around her face. "That's your problem. You think too much."

Sliding gracefully from the edge of the desk, she dropped to her knees beside Amanda's chair. Nina's hands settled on Amanda's thighs, parting them slightly.

While she knew that she should resist, Amanda found herself giving in to her lover's sensual spell. Ever since Nina had entered her life, she'd found herself utterly willing to sample forbidden delights. Nevertheless, she also knew that there was a big difference between having sex in a public bathroom and letting her lover eat her pussy in her own office.

"Let your mind rest for a bit, and just feel."

After a quick glance at the stack of papers awaiting her signature and approval, Amanda had to agree. She had been working too hard and she deserved to relax from time to time. Nodding, Amanda sank back into her chair and parted her knees. Nina settled between them, her hands slipping up Amanda's inner thighs to her panties. With a smooth movement, she jerked them down to her lover's knees.

Amanda kicked off her heels and lifted her legs, slipping free from the silk thong. Inhaling deeply, she detected a hint of her own scent in the air.

"Close your eyes."

With a soft sigh, Amanda leaned back, offering herself fully to her lover. Nina's smooth hands slowly slid her skirt up her thighs, and Amanda lifted her ass from her leather chair, allowing her to push the knee length black skirt up around her waist. Bare from her middle to her upper thighs, she couldn't contain a shiver as the cooled air in the room brushed over her heated flesh.

Pressing close, Nina reached up and under Amanda's shirt to the front clasp of her bra. Quickly, she unsnapped it, freeing her lover's breasts to press against the cool silk of her shirt. Eyes closed, Amanda lost herself in the sensations of her lover's touch; the light touch of fingertips against her nipples, the smooth feel of a palm cupping her ample breasts. Even when Nina's pinched her nipples, twisting them between her fingertips, Amanda craved more.

Amanda felt almost bereft when Nina pulled back, her fingertips dancing down her stomach to her inner thighs and on down to her knees where they paused.

Soft hair swished over Amanda's legs, moments before Nina blew softly on her quivering pussy. Trembling, Amanda gripped the arms of her chair tightly, trying to relax and let her lover lead.

Another whisper of heated breath teased her feminine flesh, followed by yet another.

Ready to beg for more, Amanda gasped instead as Nina's tongue flicked across her lips, parting her folds. Her tongue slipped past Amanda's wet lips, thrusting deep into her pussy. Pulling back slightly, she flicked her tongue across Amanda's clit, then dipped again into her moist depths.

Nina slid her hands further up her lover's thighs, then caressed the smooth shaven skin of Amanda's sex. She pressed a finger against the hard bud of her clit, and traced small circles.

Her hands dropped to Nina's hair, twisting in the

silken curls. Pulling her lover's face against her pussy, Amanda arched into the thrust of Nina's tongue. With each withdraw of the redhead's tongue, Amanda wordlessly whimpered for more. At each soft sound, Nina's tongue thrust deep within her again, only to slip free once more.

Her skin damp with sweat, Amanda slid further down in her leather chair until her ass was perched on the very edge. Tangling her fingers in the silken wave of Nina's hair, she gripped gently and lifted her legs and draped them over Nina's shoulders. Her silk shirt stretched tight across her breasts, teasing her hard nipples.

Within moments, the skilled manipulations of Nina's tongue had Amanda a quivering, shuddering mass of nerves. Nothing mattered but the delightful touch of her lover's mouth and the finger pressing against her clit.

Grinding upwards against Nina's face, Amanda's body tightened and she bit back a scream of pleasure. Intensely, the orgasm rushed through her.

Moaning softly, she breathed deeply, savouring the rippling sensations enveloping her. Every nerve in her body seemed to flair for an instant, crackling with euphoric energy.

Completely relaxed, she collapsed back in her chair. Deliciously limp, she opened her eyes and smiled as her lover licked at the juices leaking from within her core. As Nina continued to manipulate her throbbing clit, Amanda could feel another orgasm building.

A movement behind Nina and to the side caught Amanda's attention and she turned her gaze from the floor to ceiling windows along the far wall. Outside, the window washer's forehead was pressed against the glass, his cock gripped in a white-knuckled fist. His motions frantic, he came, a milky stream splattering the window.

As she watched the thick liquid cling then slid down the glass, Amanda ground her pussy into Nina's face and came again, moaning softly in pleasure.

Nina continued to lick and suck as Amanda floated down from the peak. With a satisfied smile, Nina leaned back and licked her lips. "Feeling better?"

Amanda nodded as she watched the window washer tuck his limp cock back into his pants and squeegee the window clean.

"Definitely. And I think you're right. I do need to loosen up a bit and be more daring. In fact, tonight when I get home, I want to make love to you on our balcony, and damn the risk of being watched. But first …"

Amanda paused, and leaned down to share a slow, sweet, passionate kiss with her lover. Thrusting her tongue past Nina's lips, she savoured the taste of her own come.

With a soft moan, she pulled back. She desperately wanted to sink to the floor, pulling Nina to lie down beside her, and fuck her lover senseless. But she knew that first she had a meeting to attend to.

"I need to kick you out of here, freshen up, and head to my meeting before I'm late. Tonight, we are definitely going to take advantage of our balcony."

With a tender smile, Nina stood and crossed the room. Pausing, she looked back at Amanda and blew her a kiss. Checking to make sure no one was in the outer office, she opened the door, twisted the lock, then pulled it closed behind her.

Standing on shaky legs, Amanda pulled her skirt down and re-clasped her bra. As she headed to the bathroom to brush her hair, and bring her wrinkled outfit back to some semblance of order, she watched the window washer drop to the next floor and continue about his day.

Ana's Punishment
by Tatiana Von Tauber

A tangled web has formed within the crevices of Ana's mind. Her thoughts raced with questions of morality, but lustful visions spread interwoven strands of confusion regarding her temptations. The dark allure of his suggestion prevented concentration on daily chores; Ana was consumed with his proposal. Images of erotic darkness, fear, lust, and submission lay upon her mind creating desires she embarrassingly wanted. Attempting to configure a rational for her longing to say yes, Ana played tug-of-war with the controversies in her mind, lust and honesty. She wanted to be honest in her relationship, but craved the mystery of the other man's dominance. Her emotions were torn and her values tested. However, the more she struggled with reality versus fantasy, the more she felt herself pulled into the deep abyss of unexplored waters.

After days of debate and confusion, the appeal of submission led her to make a simple call that would change her perception of love and sex. They met over coffee, talked passions, lifestyles and truths behind what was expected and hoped for. Her obsession was fuelled by her curiosity as she listened to him describe the parties and their on goings. Her interests peaked when he spoke of his playroom full of the things she had fantasised about: ropes, chains, whips, candles, restraints, and toys. Listening to him, Ana's mind raced to create the images of their use and his role in this experience, an event to surrender to her fantasies, despite the consequences of her actions.

The drive to his apartment was long. Her nerves created knots at the pit of her stomach but the reflections of the wet and empty streets created an entranced state of mind. She was hypnotized by the glow of coloured lights on the glistening road and the sound of the rain crashing onto the windshield. She wanted this, right or wrong.

The apartment walls were shades of rich chocolate brown with a simplistic décor and clean, simple lines. No complexities existed. Even the missing railing on the staircase stripped away any boundaries. They talked, laughed and stalled. Two hours had gone by and the anticipation began to irritate her very soul. She began to question if he was still serious about his proposal, yet, she found herself wondering if the time was given to her as a clean approach to reconsider. However, as the night progressed, she was unable to talk herself out of leaving.

Upon entrance into the playroom, she felt an instant, anxious arousal. The walls were a sultry red with candle sconces along its perimeter. A bed was in the corner covered with a black sheet, a swing was placed opposite the door and beside it, a large mirror reflecting back into her eyes. She stood amazed, paralysed, and excited. The room itself was an aphrodisiac. Without warning, he forced her arms behind her and threw her up against the wall. His hand came to her throat and she shuttered from excitement.

Despite the blindfold, Ana closed her eyes. She stood against the stone wall, forced to soak in the elements of its texture, rough yet partially smooth, its harsh chill digging into the nerves of her spine while her arms were suspended, clipped to the chains above her head. His breath echoed in her eardrum like the consistent rhythm of a vibrating gong, loud yet hypnotic. Breathless, bound and helpless, her eyes rolled back in desire as she began her journey into the unknown. Eternity faced her as she stood there in a curious wonder. She asked for this exploration, to be dominated, told when to listen, speak and what to do. Unexpectedly, he unbuttoned her blouse and felt his way around her body.

She stood there in awkward immobility, willing to take on the fancies of her master's teachings. Ana could not remember the words he spoke, but only her feelings of anticipation; they boiled her temptation and glorified her vulnerability. The imagery, motions and words he utilised were deliberate and measured, slow as time would be near its end. From the moment of entry into his playroom, everything was about and for her: his mental teases, his soft caresses, his poetic whispers and his pre-determined actions. He did not allow her to gratify in the pleasure of his seduction. He did not bring his hand between her legs to cool her heat, but only stroked lightly around them as to intensify her cravings. Her vulnerability became the aphrodisiac.

Suddenly, he grabbed her loose, auburn hair and forced her head back, biting into her neck. Ana's inhibitions melted but her mind raced with in fear, resistance, curiosity and shock for he promised to not hurt her. He promised a taste of this life, by Ana's request, with respect to boundaries set, but the unknown led her curiosities deeper into the murky waters of his dominance.

Ana stood bound, with the silent air broken only by sounds to interpret. She concentrated and attempted to piece the sounds to their appropriate substance. Was it a toy, another chain, a whip or simply a tease for her senses? She was led onto the bed and told to lie on her back, her arms placed above her head and her legs spread. "Do not move," he whispered.

Through the blindfold's darkness, erotic thoughts amplified and her desire for a pure rawness escalated. He hovered above her face whispering, "Do not move," once more. Her heart raced. He spoke of how difficult it was to lie still, unbound, yet subservient. "When you are tied, you can fight. It's part of the play, to try to break loose, but that becomes easy. To lie there without those ties and to be immobile is a test of your strength, submission and willpower," he said in a soft, stern tone. She found his mind game pleasingly disturbing. While Ana struggled to control her sensations, her unhooked bra was finally taken off, exposing her breasts and her vulnerabilities. She longed for his warm lips to suck upon her nipples, but instead he turned her over, pulled off her pants and exposed her ass in the thong she bought just for the occasion.

He promised only an introduction into the dark world of submission, leaving her with questions to its definition. Ana longed for him to fuck her like a master would his slave but he controlled himself, that frustrated her. He respected the boundaries they set and wondered if he would loose himself in her as she now longed for him to do. Without warning, he slapped her ass so hard she shook from its intense shock and when she verbally expressed her pain, he continued harder. He grabbed her hair as she attempted to get up. His hold was tight and empowering, permitting her submissive nature to escalate and then forced her face down into the bed. She purposefully struggled, wanting to become totally

154

overpowered by his dominance and feel like the helpless slave he promised.

When he grabbed a hold of her neck, it wasn't hard, painful or scary, just erotic. His grip sent chills up her spine; it said "obey" like nothing else. He placed an object in each one of her hands and asked her to feel them. They were cold. "One knife is real, the other is not," he whispered into her ear. Ana felt immobilised, stricken with fear yet welcomed the perversion. Unable to distinguish if the knife against her breast was real, Ana shook from excitement.

He promised safety but images raced through her mind in this game he played and she convinced herself the knife was real. Her lips chattered and her body shook. Ana tried not to analyse or think but only to feel and experience her body's reaction as it took over in fear. She was embarrassed that it provoked an erotic feeling, one so intense that her eyes rolled back in pleasure. He held her neck while lightly scraping the knife across her body. Her mind could not stop the elated feeling of her newly discovered pleasure and found she had crossed a line unknown to her. Willingly, she gave in to her master like a good slave should, begging for another encounter and another boundary to cross.

Words
by Brazilia French

The phone rings. It's him, and she's wet.

"I have a suggestion, I want your answer."

"Yes, Sir."

"An instinctive answer. I want your reaction. It matters."

"Yes, Sir." She squirms , wondering what Master has been plotting and whether her answer will come instinctively.

"I am going to buy some accessories. Cuffs and chains. I will use these as and when I see fit. It may be as restraint or punishment. The reason will however be clear. Your answer?"

"Yes, Sir."

As the phone buzzes, she realises what those two words repeated have done to her. She smiles.

Gear Stripper
by Sage Vivant

He'd heard her Harley roar into the parking lot moments before, but he acted surprised when he opened the motel room door.

"Busy?" Mischief played at Autumn's full red lips and sparked her green eyes.

"No," he smiled, moving aside to let her in. He'd been hard just waiting for her, even though he wasn't sure she'd show up. After all, he knew strippers weren't supposed to get too familiar with – what was he? Client? Audience member? Stuffer of dollar bills?

He'd seen her round breasts, her smooth, shapely ass, even got a whiff of her musky cunt when she danced near his face. He'd invited her here because now he would touch her, taste her, confirm she was real.

"We're going to do this my way, David," she explained, emptying her purse of several items he knew most women didn't normally carry. "Lie down now." She pulled a piece of rope taut between clenched fists.

She tied his ankles together. While he watched her undress, he wondered breathlessly what her plans might be for that very thick dildo that still sat on the bedspread from where it had tumbled out of her purse.

There she stood, auburn hair cascading around her shoulders. Her hips were wide and luscious. His cock stood up like a sundial as she dipped her fingers between her legs.

"Look how wet you've made me," she observed coyly, ticking his nose with her juice-coated fingers. He extended his tongue involuntarily and inhaled deeply.

"Fuck me, Autumn," he rasped.

She mounted him before he finished his request. Her moist heat hovered near his straining cock but she didn't insert him. Instead, she fed him a firm, heavy tit and commanded him to suck. Her nipple grew in his mouth.

When she'd had enough of that, she lay on his chest so he had a prime view of her glistening cunt lips. Her legs were spread wide, allowing him to watch closely as the enormous dildo slid its way up her hole. She pumped herself for a few strokes.

"Now it's your turn," she said, guiding his hand to the toy.

He did as he was told, gratefully breathing in the pussy aroma that filled the small motel room. Her honey pot dripped with sweetness. He wanted to be that dildo. Bad.

"You can fuck me now," she finally told him.

She presented her backside to him, tilting her perfect ass cheeks into the air like she was performing for a crowd. He whipped his bound feet to one side and got up on his knees. Her pussy sucked him in like he knew it would. When he pushed his entire length into her, she yelled and pushed her ass at him to drive him even deeper. They fucked like this until he came deep inside her.

As she dressed, he mumbled from the bed. "I'll have to take you for a ride on my Harley sometime."

"I can ride my own, thanks. Anyway, I've just ridden what I really wanted."

Sleepsmut
by J. Brundage

I could see her lying on the bed. She stretched, sheet barely covering her. Her eyes were closed, and she was barely asleep. I wanted to snatch off the sheet, and snatch, well, snatch her snatch. I couldn't do that just yet. I could have a little bit more fun.

I put the blindfold on her face gently. She stirred, and I took a deep breath. Luckily, she still slept. I pulled all the shades in the room, and turned on a row of old Christmas lights. Everything now had a romantic glow, yet it was bright enough to still see everything clearly. For me to see clearly, anyhow.

I decided that the sheet would stay. It was paper thin, but had a rough texture. I felt the wetness inside my lips. I brushed my damp fingers under her nose, knowing that she'd recognise the scent immediately. I saw a smile cross her face, and she stirred slightly, yet was still asleep.

"Sweetheart, it's time to wake up and have some fun," I whispered.

She just smiled, and yawned. I knew that it was time for her to be roused. If not, at least she could be *aroused*. I pressed my breasts against hers and felt nipples go as hard as mine already were. I crouched over her in a predatory squat and bit them lightly. She moaned softly. I stroked her neck, then decided to go a bit lower, tracing a path downward between her soft breasts, her abdomen, her navel, down.

I reached my destination. Her clit felt warm to the touch, even through the sheet. I pinched and pulled gently. I could see her smile widen. I held her outer lips apart with one hand, and traced all around in little circles with the other. I placed her outer lips back together, sheet still between them, moistened by her fluid.

Our smells mingled. I grabbed her outer lips with one hand, squeezing them together and pulling, rocking the sheet between them with my other hand. She moaned a little bit louder. I tore off the blindfold. Her eyes were still closed. I knew that this called for some drastic action.

I looked at the part of the sheet that was between her legs. It was damn near drenched. I could even see her pinkness through the sheet. I brushed it against my face, feeling the warmth between my own legs. I placed it back, and began stroking her. I finally plunged in with my first two fingers, thumb resting on her clit. I tickled, teased, and rocked against her until she was moaning, gasping, screaming. Her eyes popped open, and she grabbed my wrists.

"That was fun, hon," she giggled, "but just wait until *you* try to sleep!"

Smitten
by Bryn Haniver

I happened to be down at the docks that afternoon. The low sun was still bright, catching the whites of their uniforms as they came down the gangplank. I walked over to the railing and had a look.

In the middle of the line was a shock of blonde hair, thick and bobbed – she had her cap in her hand. She was petite, as all good sailors are, and even from down here I could see the vivid blue of her wide set eyes. As she came closer I noticed more: the curve of her hips under starched fabric, her easy smile as she talked with the sailor behind her, the firm swell of her breasts and the delicious sound of her laugh.

Before she got to the dock I was smitten. She gave me a curious look as she passed – I must have been staring. A bunch of them went straight for the Harbourside Tavern, so I followed.

I walked right up to her beside the bar and tried "Hey, sailor. You come here often?"

I couldn't tell if she looked disgusted or amused by the hackneyed line, but her eyes gave me a thorough once over. She got her drink and nodded towards a booth.

We sat, and I felt nervous and excited as she stared at me. Finally, she said, "Well you're fairly handsome. You might be just what a sailor needs after two weeks at sea."

Her eyes bored into mine and I felt a bit giddy. She smelled fantastic and when she put her hand over mine all the hairs on my neck stood up. I was definitely smitten.

She raised an eyebrow. "I really do hope a cat doesn't have your tongue." She leaned forward, dropping her voice to a husky whisper. "Because my pussy has other ideas."

Before I could react she pressed her drink to my lips hard, pushing my head back – I gulped it down. Whiskey, a double. I blinked a few extra times but kept my cool.

Smiling, she grabbed my arm and pulled me up out of the booth. As she headed towards the door I marvelled at the strength in her petite frame. I stumbled after her, my head swimming and my eyes locked on the graceful surges of muscle beneath the white fabric of her uniform pants.

We went to her car, parked in a special navy lot nearby, a white convertible. Depositing me in the passenger seat, she peeled out of the lot and took a back road up the hill overlooking the harbour. She swung off onto a narrow dirt track and lurched to a halt at an overlook that was hidden from the road. She got out of the car and walked to the edge of the cliff, stretching like a cat, enjoying the feel of terra firma while taking in the magnificent view of the sea.

She turned and walked back, a smile on her face as she unbuttoned those starched white pants. Sitting down on the hood of the car, she pulled them off, revealing smooth and shapely legs – and no underwear. I saw immediately that she was a natural blonde.

She tossed the pants into the back seat and then turned to face the sea. I got out of the car and walked around in front of her.

162

"I like to watch the ocean for my first on-shore orgasm," she said. Her legs parted as she spoke until they were wide open. I found myself staring at the soft pink folds she had exposed to the sun.

After a few moments she interrupted my stare. "You don't talk much, do you? I really hope your tongue is more talented at manipulation than conversation."

I grinned at that and lay down on the warm hood of the car, settling between her legs. She sighed as I licked the pale skin of her inner thighs. I used my thumbs alongside her pussy to open her as wide as I could, delighting in the soft moans she made as I did it. I held her like that for a moment, wondering how the cool gusts and warm sun felt on such sensitive skin. Finally I pressed my chin to the hood of the car, stuck my tongue into her as low as I could, and ever slowly moved it up the middle of her opened lips.

The metal of the car made creaking noises as her body shuddered but stayed in place. When I got all the way up to her clit it was engorged; I flattened my tongue against it, first lightly but then with slowly increasing pressure.

Her shuddering increased. "Move," she whispered. "Please move …" I just kept pressing. Her legs began to spasm and she grabbed the back of my head, pulling me against her even as her hips began to buck. Her ankles drummed against the hood, her back arched and a high, keening noise came from her throat. I hung on, maintaining the pressure as she went up and over.

Finally, when she sprawled back onto the windshield and her movements became quivers, I lifted my head. My chin and lips were soaked.

"God, I needed that," she groaned.

I stood, stretching sore muscles. My pants bulged, and she noticed right away.

She smiled. "I'm not sure I can stand yet," she said, twisting and rolling until she was on her stomach on the hood and her legs hung over the side towards me. She looked over her shoulder. "But I can probably help you with that anyway."

Men really are visual, and this was an exultation of whites. Puffy white clouds above. Her white convertible. The white-blond shag of hair above her navy white uniform top. And the piece de resistance, her creamy white upturned ass with two smooth white legs descending to the ground.

I knew how soaked she was and my erection practically unzipped itself. She grinned wickedly when she saw it and opened her legs a bit wider. I barely got my pants to my knees before being drawn in like a magnet, thrusting into the slippery wet heat I had prepared with my tongue.

When my hips hit her ass we both moaned and paused. I felt rigid and long, and deep inside I could feel her inner muscles fluttering against me. This wasn't going to be a leisurely fuck though – we would save that for later. It had been a long while for me as well – grabbing her hips, I withdrew a bit and began to pump.

She got her second wind quickly, squirming against the car as I increased my pace, then bucking backwards to perfectly match my rhythm. She came right away, shaking like a leaf, but it didn't slow me down and soon she was back in the beat, lunging up against me even more ferociously than before. When she began to come a third time she took me with her – my eyes lost focus in the glare of the sun and for a long moment all that existed was my cock, her slippery pussy and the squeaking of the convertible's shocks.

It was a fantastic four days of shore leave. We made

love in the car, at her place, at a campsite on the beach, even in an alley behind a nightclub. When her ship sailed again I couldn't bear to watch – we said our goodbyes in bed that morning.

Three weeks later, I happened to be down at the docks again. I spotted a shock of blonde hair coming down the gangplank. She was radiant, a supernova in a constellation of navy whites.

A voice beside me said "Mom sure looks pretty in her uniform, doesn't she Dad?"

I turned and sighed. It was never the same when Kerry, our eight year old daughter, was out of school and could meet the boat with me.

"She sure does, sweetie." I looked back at the gangplank, staring as a beautiful, familiar blonde woman descended to shore. Once again, I was smitten.

Feeling Guilty?
by Clio Knight

He wants me. We work together, we're even friends, but he wants so much more. I can tell by the careful way he always mentions his wife when we are alone together in a room. As if mentioning her makes it OK, makes this desperate sexual tension something that is not his fault. It's all about guilt, really. He drops her name into our casual conversation, telling himself that if he really wanted to fuck my brains out he would hardly be mentioning his wife, now would he?

Didn't stop him this morning, I might add.

He came around with some paperwork we had to go through before Monday. It was an awkward hour, during which we both attempted to ignore the smouldering tension. He mentioned Allie, how she was taking up tennis.

Next thing you know, our eyes had met in entirely the wrong way. Suddenly we were kissing, an old-fashioned snog with my back pressed hard against the wall and his hands madly rummaging around my bra. He shoved my skirt up around my waist, I groped at his fly and unwrapped his cock from the thin fabric of his shorts. Somewhere along the way, we snapped on a condom.

Why is a happily married man carrying condoms around with him? Curious minds wish to know.

It was a mad, rushed, entirely frantic quickie. I got a glimmer of an orgasm as his pounding, slippery penis did its thing, but just as I was getting into it he groaned and filled the condom.

After that, all that was left was guilt and embarrassment – on his side, anyway. I let him do up his pants before I pushed him out the door, but only just. I slammed it behind him, figuring that would be the end of it. No more simmering sexual tension for us, no sir.

No such luck.

He told her, of course he did. Guilty men always tell their wives eventually. Before the weekend was over, Allie was banging on my door.

I opened it and stared at the strange expression on her face. "So he told you."

She burst into a fit of laughter. "The stupid prick. Can you believe how miserable he was when he blurted it out? Those big eyes, that quivering lower lip. I think he actually expected my world to fall apart."

"You don't mind?" I asked her.

She rolled her eyes. "You know why he told me, right?"

"He was feeling guilty."

"Selfish and guilty," she corrected. "He figured the only way he would feel better about the whole thing would be to confess all, throw himself on my mercy."

I grinned. "Naturally, you would never be that selfish."

"Of course not." She met my grin with a seductive smirk. "I'd never tell him about what you and I get up to."

I chased her into the bedroom, pulled off her clothes and tongue-fucked her until she screamed. Then she worked on me, both tongue and fingers, until I came with

167

a satisfied series of gasps and groans. We nuzzled each other's breasts, licking and nibbling the soft flesh.

"Maybe I should tell him after all," she murmured, straddling me and leaning forward so I could take her nipples into my mouth, one after the other.

"Feeling guilty?" I teased as she lowered her head to kiss my throat.

"Not really," she sighed. "I was just wondering how useful he might be in a threesome."

Now, there's a thought.

Mileage
by Tom Piccirilli

I. Me And Pepito

My agent Monty Stobbs wanted me to make a pitch to one of the new twenty-something mega-producers in Hollywood. I'd moved out to LA expressly for the purpose of meeting the mover and shaker industry kids, even if they did have razor-wire moussed hair, wore steel-toed boots, and rode Harleys to lunch meetings. It seemed unduly aggressive to me but I made the effort to get over it.

The only trouble now was that this particular kid was back in Manhattan, staying at a five star hotel about thirty-four blocks from my old apartment.

"He's there setting up an urban drama for next season," Monty told me. "One of them witty Mafia shows, with the goofy hitman who cracks wise while he's digging graves behind Kennedy Airport. The teenage son of the mayor falls in love with a goombah's daughter. The mayor's trying to put her father in jail, the big boss puts a contract out on hizzoner. There's even dancing. The teens do this big number outside Lincoln Centre."

"Are their names Tony and Maria?" I asked.

Monty didn't get it. He frowned at me without catching the drift and said, "I thought you didn't read the trades."

"Christ."

"Anyway, in a week he flies off to Sicily to set up some of the Italian location shoots. You've got to catch him before then. But I can't afford a plane ticket right now. I don't see any turnaround until the Zypho units hit the video store next month. I'm tapped but I can front you bus fare. Otherwise, it comes out of your pocket."

"Monty, it was about this time last year that you were promising me a penthouse apartment on Sunset and my own private masseuse by Christmas."

"I can rub some Passionate Midnight grape-flavoured lotion into your shoulders if you want. I think I have a quarter bottle left on my night stand from when that dancer Betty the Ta-Ta Queen was here last month."

Just thinking about Betty brought a deranged expression to his face.

He saw the look in my eyes and decided not to pursue that course of the conversation.

"Consider it a tour of America," Monty said. "You'll be like Steinbeck. James Agee. Kerouac. All them road guys. You relax and look at the countryside. It'll inspire you. You'll have half the great American novel by the time you pull into Port Authority."

I didn't have quite have the energy to tell Monty that we were in the age of eight-lane interstates and telescopic, high-powered road rage. I didn't really have the energy to tell Monty anything lately.

"OK, get me the ticket."

He already had it and pulled it out of his jacket pocket. "I'll drop you off at the station. Your bus leaves at midnight."

"Jesus!"

So. Now I was on a bus with sixty other people and slowly losing my sense of reality. It was like a party where everybody hung back against the wall, didn't make a sound, and generally feared one another.

This was a four-day ride and my laptop had committed hara-kiri rather than face another minute of *Zypho II: Zyphomania-The Return of the Critter from Beyond the Edge of Space*. I got the feeling that Monty wanted a long title on the video box to cover up the picture of Zypho's less than stellar f/x. Hopefully it would edge my name off the credits as well.

I had started out writing in longhand on yellow legal pads hoping to put the time to good use, but reading my own scratchy handwriting gave me motion sickness. By the twentieth hour on the road I was trying to keep myself amused by taunting folks in the next lane to sideswipe us into a guard rail.

It was about two in the morning and I still couldn't get comfortable enough in my seat to sleep yet. I had no co-passenger beside me, but the extra space still wasn't enough for me to completely lie down. I had visions of arriving in New York after four days of insomnia and passing out in the middle of Time Square, waking up with no money, no shoes, and only one kidney.

The moonlight lent a blue haze to the darkness, and the bus' running lights were just enough to allow me to spot her one seat up on the opposite side of the aisle.

She appeared to be a part of the night, swirling, alive, as she turned to look back at me. It wasn't until I fully concentrated, focusing all my attention on her, that I saw she was a Latina woman about my age, smiling in my direction but not exactly to me.

Everyone else was asleep. She gave me the slow once-over, the kind of prying gaze that was frosty and lifeless but held a promise of distant heat. I tried to give it back to her but she ignored me. I'd never been very good at this sort of game.

She got up and silently slid into the seat beside me. I generally didn't like these kinds of wordless situations. I enjoyed words, and I hardly ever shut up. When she pressed herself to me and rubbed the meaty palm of her hand against my crotch, I began to suspect I should just shut the fuck up.

It was usually a good call.

Sometimes you had to go with the undertow. You fought your need to rationalise and argue and worry about what the real meaning was behind every act. Especially if you were going insane from boredom.

Her ragged breath blew hot against my ear. I moaned and reached for her and felt that slick electrical itch in my fingers.

"No," she said, "don't touch me."

"Uhm … but …"

"I don't like to be touched." She began to purr again, leaning into me, pressing herself into my arms while I held them out to my sides, struggling not to embrace her.

She kneeled and I crouched lower, trying to hide behind the high backs of our seats. It wasn't really working, I had nowhere to go. She tugged open my jeans and felt me through my briefs, sort of pawing, her nails lightly grazing me. I scanned the blue gloom trying to see if there might be anyone watching us, anybody else alive in the world, but the shadows became deep and edgeless as she worked me free and stroked my cock. The darkness grew heavier, inside and outside of me.

"Oh, look how cute he is … your pee-pee …" she whispered.

I checked. He didn't look cute to me at all.

"I'm going to name him Pepe … no, Pepito …!"

"Pepito? Hey –"

172

Taking my cock roughly in her hand, she brought her mouth to me and swirled her tongue around the head, slowly working down, her hands on my thighs gently patting like she was trying to urge me to her rhythm.

In the dark, I saw the glint of her eyes looking up as she pushed me farther into her mouth, now shaking her head, no no no, and drawing me out, nodding yes yes, so that her top teeth grazed and tugged at my skin.

Sometimes you want to touch somebody so badly that a fire ignites in your nerve endings and burns away your civilised self. I wanted to snarl and leave bite marks.

I heard the passengers stirring, the muffled sound of cloth on cloth as someone in front of us turned over. My hackles rose.

Continuing to pump me, she pulled me forward in the seat and pressed me back again, in control but not taking control, as she rubbed me over her face, swung my prick aside, and tongue lashed my nuts. I was so tired that I watched the scene from outside myself.

Just as I started humping against her cheek, she sucked the length of my cock down her throat. She took me in completely, clenched her lips, stared up at me, and smiled. We all had to find our pride wherever we could.

She slowly pulled herself off until only the head of my cock remained in her mouth. There was too much of a game going on here and not enough actual fun.

I reached for her hair and she growled, "Don't do that. I don't want you to do that."

I made fists and crossed my arms. I leaned back as her head bobbed over Pepito. I was trying to roll with it, to let her take me away from my utter boredom, but somehow even this was only another part of it. I was frowning in the middle of a blow job. No one would ever believe me.

She licked her palm and pumped harder at the base of my cock before taking me back in. I humped her face and lunged at her mouth erratically, and she rested Pepito near her lips and sort of crooned at him. I groaned and pressed the side of my forehead against the cool metal frame of the window. With a bitter whine, I prodded her some more, feeling my orgasm rising.

"That's it," she said. "Come on."

I jerked away and hit the frame again. There was more rustling of passengers. I bit back another moan as she sucked me wildly, her hair alive in my lap. I wanted to take handfuls of her hair and knot my grip in it and hold her in place while I cut loose. The darkness thrummed with the presence of others. I came and nearly howled in relief as she hungrily swallowed, gurgling softly, gulping as drops leaked over her lips.

I wondered if she considered my cum on her face as me touching her. I did, or thought I did, as I wafted into sleep.

It passed without dreams. I'd only snoozed for three hours but when I awoke we'd made another stop and most of the passengers seemed to have changed again. I couldn't be sure of anything much except that she was gone and I was being wilfully ignored by everybody else.

It took me a minute to realise that Pepito was still pretty much out there and waving to folks. I'd dozed off before zipping myself back up. I didn't know if anybody had seen or cared, but since I wasn't already in handcuffs I figured nobody had spotted me or had minded if they did.

Actually, he was sort of cute, I noticed, as I slipped him back home. And he remained my one and true friend in a world of quandary, and was always along for the ride no matter how many miles we covered or where the

174

bizarre journey took us.

II. Gnaw The Glass

I'd been on the bus for nearly three days and we'd pulled into more dust-choked towns and cities of smoke and steel than I'd imagined existed between the coasts. I was so tired, constipated, and restless most of the time that I just sat there in an opened-eye coma, fantasising that I was trapped in hell. For my sins, St. Peter had stuck me on a bus for all eternity. Whenever we stopped I gave a wide berth to the driver and tried hard not to call him "Pete." I imagined him with the Book of Judgment in his hands.

If there was anyone from LA still on the bus with me, I didn't know who it might be. Their faces shifted and altered from city to city. Their sighs and snores were the same, the tinny songs in their headsets and the covers of their paperbacks interchangeable. I considered setting my hair on fire just to see if anybody would notice. I was so bored that it was the only time in my life when I thought I might actually be able to stomach watching a mime. I might even join in. Walk against the wind. Pull the rope. Any damn thing.

I kept looking around, hoping to make eye contact with somebody, start up a conversation, but everyone was content in their seats, letting the miles flow over them, one after the other. I began feeling as if my skeleton was trying to make a bee-line out of my body—every muscle commenced to ache, and my temples pounded with blood. I really didn't want my obituary to read that I'd died of monotony aboard a New York-bound bus. Monty would use my death as a springboard to fame and sell my scripts for millions. He'd retire to Beverly Hills and I'd only be remembered for the

175

softcore brain juice-sucking scene from Zypho II: Zyphomania.

The twilight slowly withered to black and the smell of pine erupted. I had absolutely no idea where I was. I wondered if Steinbeck, Agee, or Kerouac had ever felt such an overwhelming loathing for cars, towns, and people in denim. The only road I wanted to write about West 4th Street in the Village. I had the sense that once I hit Manhattan I'd never leave again.

I didn't think I was lucky enough to have another woman peel herself from a section of night and come give me head. I wasn't horny but the only survival instinct I had left was the will to procreate. I felt very much the way I imagined a fruit fly might feel during its twenty-four hour life span. Do the deed and call it a day.

I scanned the sleeping passengers and spotted a blur of movement a few seats ahead.

All I could see of her in the dark was the nimbus of her blonde hair, softly glowing, and the indistinct smear of motion circling before her. I stared and studied her for five minutes before I picked up on the fact that she was masturbating in the shadows.

It got to me, but damn near anything would've.

I stood and glided up the aisle to stand over her.

You could get in trouble for doing a thing like this, but the tedium had given me an ounce of assertion. I lightly fondled her hair, then the side of her face, and stroked her neck for a moment. I held my hand out and when she took it, with her wet fingers, I drew her from her seat and ushered her back to my own.

OK, so now we were getting someplace. At least she let me touch her.

She slid past me and actually said, "Excuse me," as she passed, loosening her skirt as she took the inside spot. She slipped out of her panties and leaned against the window, reached back and clutched at my shirt, pulling me to her.

I wanted to know her name but didn't want to ask. Maybe St. Pete had stuck me in an eternal rolling orgy without intimate conversation.

She kneeled on the seat, opened her legs slightly and wriggled her ass in the dim light. Moonlight swam down and banked across her face, showing me the silver-lit silhouette.

I ground against her thigh, pressing myself tightly to her. I leaned forward and she turned and whispered into my ear, "My ass."

"Yeah?"

"Butt-fuck me."

All right, so maybe that could be considered intimate conversation. Maybe not. Sweat bloomed across my forehead and that fetid three day old stink of my own body assailed me.

I eased my index finger into her ass and crouched so that I could lick her from behind. She was wet and streaming, and I used my tongue to scoop her own juices up to her anus.

You could get funky when you had to. I slipped my finger in and worked her ass, listening to her quietly sigh, breathing soft as the sleeping passengers, the silver leaking down her back, her legs, the lovely blunt curve of her buttock. I rose and angled myself behind her, placed the head of my cock against her anus and pushed.

The air surged out of her and she made no other sound. I slid into her tightness and looked past her out the window at all the strange miles that lay behind and still lie ahead. The bus hit a bump in the road and jostled us together even more firmly, painfully, binding, as we

177

grunted in unison.

I prodded forward into her completely, then slowly pulled out, revelling in the sense that I was making, then breaking, then remaking the circuit between us. I became transparent and kind of floated out of my shoes. I thought that this is how schizophrenics must feel all the time, unanchored from the world, lost in their own misfiring neurons and too tired to care. She bucked roughly against me, spiking herself on my cock as she picked up the pace.

"That's it," she said. "Harder! Harder!"

"Jesus, be quiet …!" I hissed.

I pressed her into the window even more roughly and she climaxed and let out a titter. It took a second to realise she wasn't really getting off on what I was doing- it was the glass.

She was kissing it, licking, even biting at it. Staring into it with love and wanting. She did not care much for me or Pepito at all.

It stopped me, watching her like that. I'd gotten the vapid look in the middle of sex before-the disappointed frown, the girl calling out somebody else's name-but I'd never been thrown over for a pane of glass before.

This was the kind of thing that could shoot your self-worth to hell.

I tried to bull my way through, but I was hard pressed, slamming my cock into her from behind while the faint ghostly image of her reflection stared back at me. It was new to me, fucking a glass-licker. I suppose there'd been precedent, there always was precedent, but I'd never heard about it before.

She jammed herself backwards and I shoved into her. She moaned and ground her ass against me, thumping, even as she spread herself wider over the glass. It's amazing what can happen to you, how your guts can be plucked and knotted, but there I was butt-fucking her and growing jealous of the goddamn window.

As I thrust she reached down and fingered herself, her juice dripping between her thighs and splashing me each time I dug in. I tried to help, but she kept tilting the wrong way, angling as if she might dive headlong out of the bus. I think she climaxed but I couldn't be certain. We lived in a puzzling age. My nuts tightened and I felt no need to slow myself down and let the act linger. I'd lost her before we'd even begun, and the glass was covered with dried smears of her spit, the outline of her lips.

She murmured to the window and told it how much she loved it, shoved herself back onto me and held herself there, letting me hammer away until I came. I didn't even need to bite down on her shoulder to stifle my grunts. I had no sound to make.

She told the window, "That was wonderful. Oh god, I needed that. You were terrific."

I tried not to sigh. She dropped her skirt and passed me again saying, "Excuse me," and returned to her seat. I was a mess and didn't much care. I zipped up, sat back down, looked out on the American night and made an attempt to curb my paranoia. The glass looked on.

As soon as I caught my breath I'd head to the lavatory and get some wet tissues and wipe clean the signs of an affair I had only a minor part in. I wondered what the Book of Judgment would have pencilled in about this particular incident. Pete would not be happy. My reflection stared at me until the face of the moon grew obscured with clouds and I was thankfully left in darkness.

But the glass kept looking down at me-arrogant, vain,

and somehow sated.

III. Authority

We pulled into the Port Authority bus terminal on West 42nd Street in Manhattan, about nine AM, and while I was scrounging up my belongings the driver came back and grabbed me by the collar.

"That's unsanitary, what you been doin' right there, buddy!"

I realised then that, of course, he'd known all along what had happened, or thought had happened. "Look, Pete, nothing like this has –"

"My name ain't Pete!"

"I'm sorry, really, but –"

"Why don't you and that damn Pepito of yours get the hell off my bus before I call the cops!"

"But Pete!"

"I tole you, my name ain't Pete!"

I took my satchel, my wavering self-esteem, and my damn Pepito and dragged myself into the terminal feeling like I had detached from humanity and might not ever get back to into it.

I was so heavy with fatigue I could barely move as I lumbered among the crowd. I threw myself down in a seat and listened to the roaring bus engines outside, the thrum of the people, and tried to breathe in all the open space. Normally I'd be tracking folks all over the place, my head buzzing with dialogue and camera directions. But now I could barely remember my own name. I got up and pulled my luggage along after me like an angry child, and headed to the men's room.

It had been a hell of a trip so far, but that doomed feeling you get when serious grief is waiting around the corner hadn't left me yet. I'd had it since I was about fifteen but that didn't change matters much.

I used the urinal and spent ten minutes at the sink washing up, staring in the mirror, trying to remember what I was doing on this side of the country again. Hollywood had somehow faded off my back after five days. I felt stripped of most of the things that had kept me going day to day: ambition, desperation, fear. I was aching and exhausted but felt somehow cleansed. I was having a zen moment of tranquillity.

I saw her in the mirror and thought, okay, so this is the capper. I'd been waiting, and afterwards, I could get back on the right rail.

She came up out of the stall like the ghost of all my sins given form, and she swept behind me in one fluid motion as if she'd been meant for this and only for this. I didn't turn but stared at her reflection, trying to make eye contact. She barely acknowledged me although now she was brushing against my back. I'd described women like her in my scripts before as innocent, virginal, snow white, and the girl next door. Her bobbed blonde hair smelled of daisies. I'd never smelled a daisy before, but there it was. She was a homespun beauty that made you think of every Norman Rockwell painting, fireside family moment, Christmas morning, and endearing image that didn't actually exist in the world and probably never had.

"Spank me," she said.

I blinked a few times. I tried not to go, "uyh," but I did it anyway. I kept wondering if I was ever going to visit the good ole missionary position again with somebody I cared about.

I turned around and reached out to touch her hair. I suddenly had an overwhelming need to draw my fingers through a lovely woman's hair, to make a little contact. She dodged me without hardly even moving, as if she'd been trained for it.

"Look, lady, I'm not really feeling frisky at the moment."

Her face fell in on itself and her mouth opened and her eyes spun with pain and rejection. It took some effort for me to quell my curiosity and not suddenly rip into asking her a hundred questions on why a gold-laced girl would spend her time hiding in the Port Authority Men's Room for someone to redden her ass.

"I want you to spank me!"

"No," I told her and started to walk out.

She slid in front of me, blocked my way, tore open her shirt and pressed her tits into my face. "Bite them."

"They're very nice."

"Come on. Bite them! Chew my nipples!"

"No."

"Do it! I need to feel you."

And yet she'd eluded my touch. I'd forgotten how pushy New Yorkers could be, though I had to admit nobody'd ever quite bossed me around like this. It was a situation that locker room chest-beatings were made of. The kind of porn letters I'd send in to the low-end men's magazines for twenty-five bucks a pop.

But I'd never had to live through it before. The reality of ludicrous circumstances, plus my fatigue, was starting to make me feel drunk and dangerous. The trouble with zen moments is they vanish the moment you remember who you are.

"I'm going to kiss you," I told her.

"What?" She drew back, her frown etched in fear.

"You heard me. I'm going to make out with you. We're going to neck."

"No, that's not what I want."

"Yes, I'm taking you on a date. To the movies. And

182

we're going to sit in the back row and feed each other popcorn!"

"No!"

There was a sudden mad rush of energy and anger that knotted between my shoulders. "I'm going to kiss you and tell you how much I love you!"

"Oh God! No!"

"Bow down before Pepito, baby!"

"You're fuckin' nuts!"

"Tremble before my damn Pepito!"

"Help!"

Of course I was out of my head, but I didn't feel bad about it anymore. Sometimes your confusion made more sense than all the logic you'd build up for yourself. I leaned in to kiss her with visions of a house in the suburbs and three flaxen-haired children writhing through my heated mind. My lips brushed hers and she hauled back her fist and clobbered me.

"Get away, you freak!"

She ran out of the men's john and I stood there with my back against the stall, tasting blood against my teeth. It was just the way of things. I didn't feel relaxed or inspired. I didn't have half the great American novel written. I checked my watch. I had just enough time to get where I was going. I made it out onto 42nd street and headed for the five star hotel.

It took me twenty minutes. The desk gave me the room and I walked in on the new twenty-something mega-producer in Hollywood, with his razor-wire moussed hair, the steel-toed boots, and a handsome sneer that was supposed to make men respect him and women flush with giddiness.

We stared at each other for a minute. He started telling me all about the Mafia show and somewhere after the fourth time he said "goombah" I stopped listening.

I said, "Can I borrow your phone?"

Maybe he was struck by my audacity. He gave a self-serving grin and said, "Sure."

I called Monty and said, "Monty, I'm not coming back. I'm out of this game."

"But ... but – wait! What about the movie?"

"Zypho and his love tentacles are going into retirement. See you around."

"You can't! Wait, let's talk ...!"

I clicked off, handed the kid his phone back, and decided to sit in Central Park for the rest of the afternoon. I had nowhere to go, but I didn't mind. I was back in control.

Lacy
by Jolie Du Pré

It was late evening, and Regina was still at her desk staring at the pile of papers waiting for her review. Lacy had to be told. Her modelling gigs had dried up, and she hadn't worked in months. She wasn't looking for jobs, either. While Regina worked long hours at Davis and Keller, Lacy sat in Regina's apartment wasting away the hours in front of the tube.

Regina Walker had graduated summa cum laude from Northwestern University and with honors from Harvard Law. Written up in the Chicago Tribune Magazine as one of the city's rising young African American lawyers, she was going places. Her salary had increased substantially, giving her the opportunity to afford the Gold Coast apartment she rented. So what was she doing with Lacy? The woman never washed a dish or picked up after herself. Even worse, the smell of pot often permeated the living room at the end of the day.

Regina had been hooked on Lacy Brown the moment she had laid eyes on the young woman's shapely figure sashaying down Michigan Avenue.

"You starin' at me?" Lacy had asked.

"Ah, no, miss."

"I saw you at that lesbian fest. You was talkin' on stage, right?"

Regina thought back to the coffeehouse where she had been a speaker. "Yes,

that was me."

"Yeah, I thought that was you." Lacy had looked Regina up and down, which had sent a chill through Regina's core. "You hungry? I'm hungry."

Regina wasn't hungry, but Lacy was, and Regina knew an opportunity when she saw one. At a cozy restaurant, they dined on pasta and drank white wine.

"I'm a model around here. Have you seen me before?" Lacy asked.

"I don't believe I have," Regina said, "but I'm certainly enjoying the view."

Two hours later, Regina had Lacy in her bedroom and it was Lacy she was eating.

Lacy stayed that night and then the next. Soon she had become a permanent fixture in Regina's apartment.

It had all begun a year ago and now it had taken its toll. Regina rose from her desk to stand in front of the mirror that hung on her office wall. She put a finger to her hair, twisting a strand of her dark locks. The whites of her eyes were turning red and the brown skin around them had developed a few wrinkles.

The McNamee case involved a huge chunk of her time and she didn't need worries about Lacy anymore. She grabbed her purse, left the papers on her desk and headed home. Work would have to wait until morning. Lacy had to be told.

"How are you, Miss Walker?" asked the security guard when Regina entered her apartment building.

"I'm hanging in there Charlie, thanks. Did Lacy leave at all?"

"I haven't seen her, ma'am."

Of course not. She hadn't left. She had been in the

apartment all day, like always.

Regina took the elevator to the 18th floor. She fumbled for her keys and then opened her door.

"Hi, baby," Lacy sat on the kitchen counter facing Regina, naked.

"Jesus, Lacy! What are you up to now?" Regina began to feel the throb between her legs that she couldn't control. There was Lacy. Her thick, wavy hair flowed down her caramel shoulders to her ripe, full breasts. The snake tattoo that began on her firm stomach angled down to her shaven pussy between her spread legs.

"I been waitin' here for you baby. I know you had a hard day."

Regina closed the door and inhaled the faint smell of pot that correlated with the daze in Lacy's eyes. "You've been smoking, Lacy. You know I don't like that." Regina tried to look firm, tried to look dead into her eyes, but her own eyes trailed to Lacy's full breasts and to her bald pussy that glistened between her caramel thighs. She wanted to run away, run out the door and have Lacy removed somehow. But the throbbing between her legs, the throbbing for Lacy, was stronger now.

Placing her briefcase on the floor, Regina slowly walked over to Lacy. She kissed her lightly on the lips and then tried to back away. But Lacy pulled her closer. Regina stared into Lacy's green eyes and soon melted, covering her lips with her own and darting her tongue into her mouth.

Lacy grabbed Regina's head and shoved her mouth on her hardened nipple.

Regina took Lacy's breast in her hands, sucking hard and madly.

"Mmmmm," Lacy moaned as Regina put the other breast in her hands. The sweat from Regina's body began

187

to soak her shirt as she buried her face into Lacy's chest.

Regina ran her fingers down to Lacy's smooth pussy and entered her. Lacy was dripping and Regina was so aroused that she was almost blinded. She dropped to her knees in front of the counter, ripping her stockings a bit as she plunged her tongue into Lacy's pussy.

Could any woman ever taste this good? Regina spread Lacy's thighs wide, covering her folds with her lips and tongue. She wanted her juices all over her face. She wanted it, all of it. Bending Lacy back, Regina brought Lacy's ass in front of her face. *I'm going to bite this bitch until it hurts*, Regina thought. Lacy pushed her bottom against Regina's lips, moaning to orgasm with the bites of Regina's mouth.

Afterwards, Lacy lay on the counter exhausted and saturated. Regina, wet and dishevelled, rested her head on Lacy's stomach.

"I want you to leave," Regina whispered.

"I know. You told me before. But I don't wanna go. I love you. Don't you love me?"

Regina rose off of Lacy and stood up. It was true. She had said that before.

"I love you, Lacy, but I'm tired of carrying you. You've got to do something with your life. You're an attractive woman. Get back out there and model again."

"I know. I'm tryin'."

"No, you're not. If things don't change, you're going to have to leave."

"OK baby, OK. I'm gonna clean up now, OK? You want some dinner?"

"Yes, Lacy. I suppose that would be fine." Regina lifted her briefcase and carried it down the hall to her bedroom. Lacy turned on the radio and sang with the music as she began to pick up what she had laid around.

"Lacy, turn it down. It's too loud!" Regina shouted.

"Sorry, baby. I'm sorry."

Regina turned to glance at Lacy's naked body. Lacy held her hair in her hand as she cleaned, her firm ass bent over to reveal her shaven and now satisfied pussy, her full breasts bouncing with each movement.

God, Lacy, why are you so damn beautiful? Regina sighed. Turning her eyes away, Regina walked into her bedroom and closed the door.

She Knew
by Clare Moore

She knew that she was going to get screwed.

She'd helped him pick out his clothes for his new job. She'd helped with three jackets and five pairs of pants, and about six shirts. He had been back a couple of times in the last two weeks. She'd helped him put on and take off jackets. She'd measured his inseam, and his shoulders, and chest.

On his third visit, he didn't bother going in to the dressing room to change pants. He just dropped them there in front of her, and stood in his tight boxers. It was probably then that she went a little higher in his crotch when he was trying on another pair of pants. She touched his balls with the back of her hand, and kept on measuring.

He began to get bigger, and he turned away, embarrassed.

He paid for his selections, and asked her out, for Friday after the shop closed; for tonight. She knew she was going to get screwed. She thought about it all day. She thought about when it would happen, and where. She thought about what she should wear, so it would be easy for him, with a simple dress that would lift over her head in a flash, showing maybe a black lace bra.

Maybe a soft satin blouse with a hundred buttons, so

190

that it would take forever to open her up, with only a tee under it. She hadn't decided when she dressed in the morning, and now had only about an hour before he would walk in the door.

You had to wear the right clothes for a first screw. It was just a matter of how long should it take, and how hard to get there. The last customer had long left. She had to decide.

By the time the bell rang over the door as he walked in, she was ready. She was standing in the middle of the three dressing mirrors, so he saw her from front, back, and sides. She stood with her hands on her hips, and her legs apart, in a mannequin pose.

He stopped when he saw her, and crossed his arms as he stood there and took her in from bottom to top.

Brown wing tip shoes over black over-the-calf socks.

Very snug pleated and creased dark blue trousers with a faint pin stripe.

No belt.

Dark blue suspenders, buttoned to her pants, and tight against her chest.

A matching blue double-breasted jacket, buttoned.

A thin elegant white striped shirt, buttoned up to her neck.

A tight white armless striped undershirt, over her bare breasts.

And a silk blue and maroon print tie, properly tied, hanging down her front.

No bra. And silk boxers. Black.

She was going to get screwed, but wanted it different. And wanted it to take time. He walked up to her. She pulled the curtain in front of the mirrors closed. She reached into her inside breast pocket and took out a deck of cards. She held them out to him in the palm of her hand.

He cut the deck. 7.

She cut it. 4.

She took off her jacket. One hardened nipple slipped from behind the suspenders, and pushed out the shirt.

He cut. 10.

She. Jack.

She removed his jacket for him, and hung it on the hook. It was one she had sold him.

Next his belt. He insisted it was not part of his pants.

Her shoes.

Her socks.

His tie, his shoes, his socks.

He cut. King!

Ace!

He started to unbutton his shirt. She unfastened his pants instead. He dropped them, and stepped out of them. He was bulging in his boxers. It was down to his boxers and shirt. She had her tie, suspenders, shirt, pants, and underwear.

His shirt!

He took the deck, and shuffled it. He stepped back off the platform, and sat in the dressing room chair, in only his boxers. He drew a card, not looking at it, and tossed it toward her. It landed on the platform face up. 3.

He drew another card, and without looking at it, held it up for her to see: 5.

He got up, went to her, and untied her tie, brushing against her breasts as he removed it.

He went back to the chair, and tossed her a 9. He held up a Queen. He pointed to her pants. She pointed to her suspenders, shrugged, and slipped them to her sides. Both nipples were hard.

8. 9. She started to unbutton her shirt, slowly, then

pulled it out of her pants, then pulled the shirt open to reveal her breasts, and slipped the shirt off. He started throbbing in his boxers.

She walked over to him, and drew a card. Ace. He drew. Ace! He held the deck to her. She slowly shook her head, and unfastened and dropped her pants. She stepped back, and pointed to the mirrored platform.

He walked to it, shaking his head. Facing the mirrors, he slid his boxers down, and kicked them off the platform. He didn't turn around. She could she him, erect, from three views. He shook his head, and put his hands on his hips, and turned around, stepping off the platform.

He drew one last card. The 4th ace. He held it up for her to see. She knew she was going to get screwed. She knew it was going to be now. He slipped off her silk boxers, and grabbed her in his arms, and pushed her back against the mirrors, and thrust himself into her.

Cramped Booths And What They're Good For
by Lynne Jamneck

She glanced over her shoulder as we entered the park, eyes beckoning me into a booth at the far end of the park.

You've seen those teeny little red telephone boxes – a tight squeeze at best.

I followed her inside.

And yes, her ass was super, super tight.

I grabbed it immediately and hoped the booth wouldn't fall over as I slammed her against the grimy glass panelling. It didn't fall over, but made a fucking racket nonetheless.

Thank god it was dark.

Her tongue tasted of cigarettes and cinnamon – those shooters she'd been chugging like a champion back at the bar.

She was one of those girls who used kissing as foreplay:

Look, see? This is not only what my tongue can do in your mouth, but to other parts of your body too if you'll let me.

She bit my lips, top and bottom; licked them, sucked roughly on my tongue.

Took my one hand from her tight little derriere and slid it underneath the stretchy Daddy's Girl T-shirt she was wearing.

Christ – she had tits that made me think of double-edged chocolate. A creamy and smooth, white base, with dark cocoa-topped nipples.

Her hot cheek against mine, she moved her lips to my ear: "You're some cock of the walk, aren't you?"

"And you're the type who likes that," I said.

"Aren't you fucking clever. Now get to work."

Swiftly, removing my hand from underneath her clothing I grabbed her hips and spun her round. She exclaimed something unintelligible, her open hands slamming hard against the glass.

But she liked it. Her body begged me.

She tried to say something but I ground my teeth and told her to shut her mouth.

She listened, motivate I'm sure by the veracity of my command and the simultaneous fear that I would stop if she disobeyed. I knew her type well. When it came to foreplay she was all over you. But with the foreplay over, she relinquished her own aggressiveness for the more passive part.

There was no time to waste. I'm terribly paranoid by nature, and my fatalistic thinking already saw tight-lipped Bobbies carry both of us off to the nearest police station.

Book 'em Boyo: indecent exposure.

If I was going to fuck her, I'd better do it quick. Quick, but thoroughly.

I reached round, fingers fumbling at the buttons of her fly, then gave her jeans a good yank. An echo of lust cracked in her throat. I grabbed a handful of her dirty-blonde hair, at the same time stealthily thrusting two fingers inside her. Her back arched, sending her perfect ten ass into my crotch.

My phantom dick rejoiced.

And to think, it all coalesced into instantaneous lust at the corner bookstore:

"Your face looks awfully familiar," was how she decided to split the ice.

"I'm a writer."

"No, that's not it."

"Bugger."

Conveniently, she kept quiet.

Save for the quiet unh-ahh sounds she kept making into the finger-smudged glass. Thank god she refrained from shouting something like "Jesus Christ fuck me!" or our collective asses would've been cooked for sure.

Without removing my fingers, I turned her round to face me, smiling at the thought of her naked cheeks against the cold glass. At the same time, I tried keeping an eye out for the approaching right arm of the London law, but the way her lips only mouthed the words I wanted to hear out loud was somewhat of a distraction, nonetheless.

– Deeper –

was one of them.

– Harder –

of course, was another.

– Slower –

came tumbling after, which I wouldn't give to her yet, and pleasingly served to make her even harder and wetter in my hand. In my opinion, that certainly was homage enough to my technique. So then I relinquished, and indeed did fuck her slower, yet still with some force and little restraint.

When I looked down I saw her jeans halfway down her pretty thighs, arousing me even further. I pulled her into me while she rode my hand like a cowgirl trying to prove something.

The second time we happened into one another was at the chic dyke bar where I moonlight as bartender. Just two hours ago to be exact.

"You made me so hot, strutting behind that bar counter."

The actual sound of her voice made my head swim delightfully. The air around us, trapped in the confined space of the telephone booth became humid as we repeatedly breathed it in and out again. In and out. Faster. It was turgid, unmoving, recycled hot air and smelled of spent sex.

"And you're a cock tease," I grinned.

"Which you get off. Get off on –"

"I'll admit: I had lurid visions of screwing you in that dingy bar toilet."

"'Oh Jesus."

I held my hand steady as her hips increased their tempo, pulsing to a desperate rhythm, hell-bent on satisfaction.

"So that's your dish. Rich daddy's girl who likes to get fucked by blue-collar dykes."

"Oh, god."

Nailed it – hammer on the proverbial nail. I'm an excellent judge of character. Being a writer helps to know what drives people. She probably had a girlfriend who wasn't aggressive enough in bed – I could see that particular exasperation behind her eyes – the need, the hunger.

"Fuck, I'm gonna come."

"I'd be disappointed if you didn't," I replied through my own personal bliss.

Orgasmo mundo struck, and she bit my neck because she had to do something to refrain from bellowing and

197

alerting the whole block as to what we were doing.

Dogs began to bark.

Who the fuck walked dogs this time of night?

"Pull up your pants, darling," I whispered fiercely.

"First you fuck me, then you order me around?" she stumbled. "Isn't that what I have a girlfriend for?"

We stumbled out the booth in opposite directions. I headed straight into Burger King.

Hopefully they still had a whole cow on one of the racks.

Thank god she never told me her name – that could've spoiled everything.

Pity I never found out why my face looked so familiar.

Suffice to say – next time she sees me in a bookstore, she'll remember.

Why Can't I Be You?
by Alison Tyler

Sounds silly, I guess, but sometimes when I see him, I don't want to fuck him, I want to *be* him. Matt has the perfect male body, in my opinion. Broad-shoulders, a long, lean torso, slim hips, and an amazingly awesome ass. He has a deeply fuckable body, and I do love to fuck him. But sometimes I don't want him to climb on top of me and pound into me, don't want him to bend me over and take me from behind, don't want him to press me up against the wall and make me writhe with pleasure.

No, what I want is to slide inside him and see the world from within his head. And I want to devour some summertime chicklet dolled up in one of those swishy floral dresses and tie-up espadrilles and fuck *her* while being him.

Too much like that John Malkovich movie?

Maybe.

But why can't I be him? Just for an evening. Or even for an hour. Why can't *I* be the one to move through the crowd and pick up a girl, any girl? (He can have any girl.) Why can't I take one home, or out to some back alley, and push her up against the brick wall out there, tear her panties down and fuck her?

That's all I want. One hour. One hour inside of his body so that I can find out what it's like – not just to be a man, but to be *him*. I want to manhandle my throbbing cock, to hold it, to fondle it. I want to force-feed every inch of it to some pretty, summertime chicklet, to make her drink me, and drain me. To make her feel my power.

He's not always that type, I know. He is sweet and caring and gentle. He is monogamous and dedicated to me. But *I'd* be that type if I were him. I'd be the type to control the situation. I'd be the type to take charge. It would feel good to take charge. God, it would feel amazing.

My vision gets to a point where I am all-consumed by the thought. So I take one step forward, or really one roll forward on the mattress, and I curl my body up next to his in bed, and I say, "I have a fantasy …"

He slides one strong arm around me, holding me close. "Tell me, baby," he whispers back, the way he always does. He likes my mind best. More than my ripe, lush breasts. More than my thick, black hair. More than the curves of my hips or the swell of my ass, he likes my thoughts. My dirty fantasies. My X-rated visions. "Tell me where your mind is going tonight," he croons in his low, husky voice.

"I want …" I start, but I can't say it.

"Tell me."

"No," I whisper, shaking my head.

"Tell," he says, and his voice is insistent.

"I'll show you," I decide. Because that will work best.

"Show –" he starts, but I put my finger to his lips, and without another word, I climb out of bed and grab the satchel containing my outfit and all my recently purchased gear, and I disappear into our bathroom. I can almost hear his thoughts going crazy in the other room – *where is she going? What's she doing?* – but I pay more attention to my own thoughts. At this point, they're all that matter.

I gaze at myself as I bind my breasts flat with an Ace bandage. I admire my body as I slip into the recently purchased harness and adjust my fine, handsome cock. I slide into the faded 501s, and put on the boots, and add a wife-beater T-shirt that makes my arms look cut and fierce.

Who am I?

Will he know?

I gel my hair and tuck my ponytail up into a cap, then slip on a pair of his shades. I can see it. I can feel it. I add cologne, from the expensive bottle I bought him last Christmas, and then I walk back into our bedroom and wait to see what his response will be.

"Oh, Jesus," he sighs when he sees me, and I know with that ripple of pleasure that runs instantly through me that he's game. "Oh, *god*," he says, looking me up and down. I'm tall and lean and hard. My hand is already on my belt. I want to undress as quickly as I wanted to dress. But first, I have to strip him down. I have to oil him up. I have to kiss him all over, lovely flower that he is. Because now that I'm him, well, who does *he* have to be?

We don't need to answer that question, do we? I didn't think so.

Even though I feel like being naked so he can really see the transformation, I don't take off my clothes this time. I need him too fast for that. I part my jeans and let him admire my cock. I manhandle my cock, my fist wrapped tight. I want to slide it across his pretty lips. I want to watch him deep throat it.

He wants that, too.

"Look," I say. "Get close so you can see me. Really see me."

He scrambles on the bed to obey. His mouth is open

201

before I can command it. I don't have to tell him what to do. His lips part, and he takes me in. I feel him pulling on my cock. I feel how hungry he is for that. I envision him draining me, taking me all the way to climax with the sucking motions of his ravenous moth.

Later. *After*.

For now, I push him back. There's lube in the drawer by the bed. Usually, it's lube for me. Now, it's lube for him. I tell him to get me the bottle, and then I let him watch me grease myself up.

"You know where this is going," I say, seeing his eyes widen, seeing him bite hard on his bottom lip, as if he might want to say something, but doesn't quite dare. "You know," I say, softer, but I can tell from the rosy blush on his face that he understands. Of course, he does. Then I roughly roll him over on the bed, and pull his boxers off, and spread those lovely asscheeks of his, and kiss him there between them. Mmm. I take my time, the way he takes his time, and I can tell as he grows more aroused from the way he shifts against the sheets.

He likes this. My baby likes this.

I oil him up, so gently, so sweetly, my fingers going deep inside of him, and while my fingers work slowly into his asshole, I press my face against his smooth skin and breathe in deep. Oh, is he sweet. He is my angel. My lover. My sweet young thing in a floral dress and tie-up espadrilles, so ready and willing to get fucked against some back-alley wall.

I sit up on my haunches, and I get ready to plunge. My baseball cap comes off, but my hair stays in place, and I'm still him as I work the first part of my thick, ready cock into his asshole.

And as I fuck him, I realise that we've blurred, because there I am in the mirror. There I am. But who am

I? And there he is, his expression one of awe and surrender. And who is he? And more important than either of those questions is this one: Does it matter?

No. Not at all.

Not tonight.

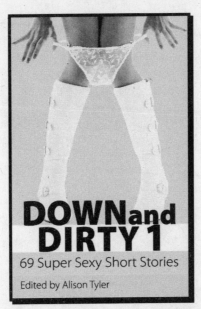

Down & Dirty - volume 1
Edited by Alison Tyler

The short stories in this collection are written by some of the best authors in the business—including M. Christian, Thomas S. Roche, Sage Vivant, Maxim Jakubowski, Rachel K. Bussel, N. T. Morley, Dante Davidson, and many more. Some stories are sensational sexual snippets, while others are fully detailed dramatic depictions. All of the 69 pieces have one thing in common: They're dirtier than dirty. And we know that's just the way you like them!

Violet Blue, Good Vibrations
"When we're in Tyler's world, our senses go into overdrive."

Aromancereview.com
"Editor Alison Tyler has done a wonderful job of picking out a fabulous variety of stories for this volume."

ISBN 9781906125806   Price £7.99

Juicy Erotica
Edited by Alison Tyler

Food and sex are fiercely entwined in many people's fantasy repertoires. Who hasn't bitten into some deliciously indecent dessert and felt those familiar flutters of pure ecstasy? And aren't those flutters similar to sexual sensations? Of course, we're talking about only the best desserts...and the best sex, which is exactly where the concept for this anthology began. Alison Tyler wanted to gather a collection of the juiciest tales, food-related, and sex-infused to share with those whose fantasies meld with her own.

ISBN 9781906125875   **Price £7.99**

The True Confessions of a
London Spank Daddy

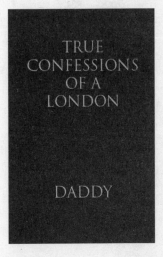

My name is Peter, I'm 55 and I'm a Spank Daddy. I offer a spanking and disciplining service to women...

Discover an underworld of sex, spanking and submission. A world where high-powered executives and cuddly mums go to be spanked, caned and disciplined.

In this powerful and compelling book Peter reveals how his fetish was kindled by corporal punishment while still at school. How he struggled to contain it until, eventually, he discovered he was far from alone in London's vibrant, active sex scene.

What he learnt on the scene helped him to understand the psychology of women who wanted to submit to submissive discipline. Many were professional women, often juggling a demanding job and family. They needed to occasionally relinquish all control, to submit totally to the will of another. Others sought a father figure who could offer them the firm security they remembered from their childhood when Daddy had been very much in control.

Chapter by chapter he reveals his clients' stories as he turns their fantasies into reality. The writing is powerful, the stories graphic and compelling.

Discover an unknown world...

ISBN 9781906373313   Price £9.99

Ultimate Burlesque
Edited by Alyson Fixter
& Emily Dubberley

Raising money for breast cancer
All profits go to Macmillan Cancer Care

Enter the sparkling world of burlesque as you've never seen it before. The UK's top erotic writers revel in the erotic glamour of fluttering eyelashes, twirling tassels and more than a hint of stocking.

Sapphic encounters, fetish fun, sensual exploration, kinky submission and domination – whatever your pleasure these stories are guaranteed to provide the ultimate tease.

20 erotic short stories with a burlesque twist introduced by Chris Manby and featuring writers including Katie Fforde, Jo Rees, Olivia Darling, Nikki Magennis, Maxim Jakubowski, Kristina Lloyd and Lauren Wissot.

ISBN 9781906373634   **Price £7.99**

Also from Xcite Books

Sex & Seduction	**1905170785**	**price £7.99**
Sex & Satisfaction	**1905170777**	**price £7.99**
Sex & Submission	**1905170793**	**price £7.99**
5 Minute Fantasies 1	**1905170610**	**price £7.99**
5 Minute Fantasies 2	**190517070X**	**price £7.99**
5 Minute Fantasies 3	**1905170718**	**price £7.99**
Whip Me	**1905170920**	**price £7.99**
Spank Me	**1905170939**	**price £7.99**
Tie Me Up	**1905170947**	**price £7.99**
Ultimate Sins	**1905170599**	**price £7.99**
Ultimate Sex	**1905170955**	**price £7.99**
Ultimate Submission	**1905170963**	**price £7.99**

www.xcitebooks.com